THE DOUBLE AXE

Philip Womack

BOOK ONE

OF THE

BLOOD AND FIRE

SERIES

ALMA JUNIOR

ALMA BOOKS LTD
3 Castle Yard
Richmond
Surrey TW10 6TF
United Kingdom
www.almajunior.com

The Double Axe first published by Alma Books Ltd in 2016

© Philip Womack, 2016

Cover design: Jem Butcher Design

Printed in Great Britain by CPI Group (UK) Ltd, Croydon CR0 4YY

ISBN: 978-1-84688-390-3
eBook ISBN: 978-1-84688-401-6

TO MY SON,
ARTHUR WOMACK VON PREUSSEN

Author's Note

While I have used a map of the palace at Knossos as a template for that which Stephan and his family inhabit, scholars disagree about the function of each room, so I've found it more helpful to think of the palace as an imaginary space in which the myth happens. It isn't "real", or "historical": simply a framework on which to stretch a story, like a tapestry.

For clarity, I have employed the Greek names for the main characters that have come down to us in the received myth: Minos, Pasiphaë, Ariadne, Theseus. Theseus's companions have names from Greek poetry.

Minos, according to legend, had several children, one of whom was called Deucalion: I have imagined him as my hero, Deucalion Stephanos.

I have, of necessity, invented some characters; a couple have names that come from a Minoan tablet (Bansa, Rusa); others I've given Greek names that felt appropriate to their function and character (Timon, Myrrah, Lysias, Lords Callias and Nicodemus.)

Myths are elastic: this is simply my version, another way into the great store of stories that is Greek mythology.

– Philip Womack

PRONUNCIATION GUIDE

Deucalion Stephanos– Dew-*kay*-lee-on *Stef*-an-os

Ariadne – A-ree-*ad*-nee

Minos – *Mine*-os

Pasiphaë – *Pas*-if-ay

Daedalus – *Dee*-dal-us

Icarus – *Ick*-ar-us

Myrrah – *Mirr*-a

Timon – *Ti*-mown

Theseus – *Thee*-see-us

Philoclea – *Fil*-o-klay-a

THE DOUBLE AXE

1

MYRRAH'S CURSE

Before anyone had even heard of the Minotaur, before Myrrah uttered her terrible curse, we were out hunting a white hind in the forest. The hounds, led by my favourite, Patch, found her scent immediately.

We were galloping along, the branches of cypresses waving against the brightening sky. I was keeping close to the front, so they could say that I, Prince Deucalion Stephanos, had ridden bravely.

That was my full title. Most people, though, called me Stephan. I preferred it.

I was riding my grey mare, Swift, and I jumped a stream at the same time as my father, King Minos, on his black stallion, Farseeker, and I caught an expression of pure joy in his face. He shouted out and surged ahead, so I spurred Swift on. Hunting was something we both loved.

"Imagine you're drawing the sun's chariot, not carrying stupid old me!" I whispered to Swift. Silly, I know, but I liked to talk to her. She whickered and flicked her ears, as one of the huntsmen came up to us on his horse and my father sped on.

"She's going up by the Black Lake, towards the mountains!" he cried.

Timon, my father's steward, came panting up behind me. He was having trouble controlling his stallion. Timon's face was shiny with sweat. He was wearing a crimson-tinged tunic, with gold glinting on his fingers.

"You are enjoying yourself, prince?" he simpered.

I nodded curtly.

"Your brother Androgeos would have been far ahead by now," Timon continued. "He'd have scented the hind himself, he had such a good nose!"

I kicked Swift's flanks, holding on to her mane; she whinnied and hurtled on. The feel of the hunt was filling my blood, and Timon's veiled taunts were angering me. I could do as well as Andro. He was away, over the Middle Sea to the north, on the mainland, staying at the court of King Aegeus of Athens. I would be as good as him.

I overtook my bodyservant, Bansa, who'd somehow got ahead of me on his young mare. Bansa laughed as

I went by. "The hind! She's white as milk!" he shouted. "Clever too."

I grinned at him.

I spotted Farseeker and my father, and urged Swift on. As I came up beside him, he turned his head and gave me a joyful smile. "Ahead!" he cried.

My father was full of the fire of the hunt. We thundered onwards through the trees, and I did my best to stay just behind him.

I was thirsty. My spear was heavy in my right arm. Bansa had forgotten to give me a water bottle and I hadn't drunk anything since the wine at the start of the hunt.

The baying of the hounds became louder, and we came out to where a small waterfall trickled down the rocks.

There was a circle of hounds – Patch, his little throat quivering with sound, and Keen, and Bounce – all eagerly barking.

Our quarry, the hind, was at bay. She couldn't get up the rocks, and she was hemmed in on all sides.

She was larger than was usual for her age and sex. Her head was raised up and, like a swan, she was pure white.

I'd never seen anything like her before – so beautiful, like a creature of moonlight.

Suddenly, I didn't want to hurt her. She was frightened, exhausted. She skittered from side to side, and jumped back, scared by the string of red feathers that the men had placed in the trees to frighten her. The dogs were barking, their jaws gaping, snapping at the air, as she evaded them.

The sun was high, and it gleamed off her flanks. There were men hidden behind the trees, waiting with nets – but now I wanted her to run, to escape.

"The prince should take the first throw!" shouted Timon.

I looked at my father. He nodded.

Bansa stood transfixed. "As white as the moon!" he said, eyes staring.

"Come on prince!" called Timon. He was beside me now. The dogs were yapping, the hind trapped.

I could feel all the men looking at me, their horses restless, their eyes keen.

The hind was slow and tired now. She could barely move. Her body was slack and the dogs were nipping at her.

A huntsman raised his arm and I took that as a challenge, lifting my spear. My aim was good. I could get her in her flank, in the heart, in the best place. Behind me Timon was whispering – more remarks about Andro, perhaps. Hefting the spear above my head I heard my father's shouts of encouragement and all the men roaring and the whole clearing ringing with noise.

For a second she lifted her head up to me and I looked into her eyes.

I couldn't hold that milky gaze. I threw the spear, blindly. There was a pause, in which I could only make out a single dog's bark: it was Patch.

And then the men shouted. Through their cries I heard the hind's moan of pain. I looked up, barely wanting to see.

Timon was clapping his hands. My father was shaking his spear in triumph.

I'd got her. I'd got the hind. The thought seared through me, making my whole body tingle. I'd got the hind.

My spear was sticking out of her flank. The blood was spotting her whiteness. She staggered and fell to her knees, and the other huntsmen went in to finish the job, the dogs awhirl around them.

My father rode up to me and clapped me on the back. "A fine shot, Stephan!" he said. "Fit for a prince!" He grabbed my arm in congratulation.

His approval washed over me. But somewhere inside me, I also felt sick. I'd killed that animal, that beautiful creature, and maybe we would never see anything like her again.

"Stephan!" shouted Minos, and the men took up the cheer. As they shouted my name, excitement and pride spread through me to see them all standing around me, some holding nets, some with knives, while the dogs pestered the hind's corpse, waiting for their reward. I was elated.

The men cheered once more, then slowly returned to their tasks. My father stayed with me for a second.

He was about to say something, when a sharp, wailing sound, like the lamentation of women at a funeral, chilled the clearing. At first I thought it might be the hind giving out its final cry, and my stomach twisted. But it couldn't be. The keening was much, much harsher than anything a hind could produce, more harrowing than anything I'd heard at a funeral. My father released my arm. He turned round, slowly and deliberately. Swift shivered beneath me.

From out of the trees, into the clearing, came a woman, screaming.

"Who is she?" someone said.

Tall and veiled, she was shouting something I couldn't understand. She tore off her veil and it floated away from her into the trees. Everything paused.

"It's Myrrah!" cried a voice. "The priestess. She lives by the Black Lake!"

We had passed her house on the way – a low, wooden thing, smoke billowing out of the roof. I hadn't given it a moment's thought.

The entire crowd of hunters fell silent. The dogs, cowed, turned away from the hind. The huntsmen's hands were dripping blood.

Only Myrrah's insistent screams pierced the air.

Now I could make out a word – a name, among the screams. "Dictynna… Dictynna!"

Dictynna – the hunt goddess. She was calling the name of the hunt goddess.

My father got off his horse and handed me the bridle. He walked calmly through the crowd of hunters. I dismounted as well, and gave the horses to one of the huntsmen to tend.

My father and I went right up to Myrrah. Only then did she stop wailing, and the silence rang like thunder. Her black hair was uncoiled, hanging loosely around her face.

"Violation!" Myrrah screeched. "Dictynna is violated! The white hind is killed…"

My heart jumped in my breast. Now I was so close to Myrrah, I could see her clearly. Her face was frozen, and the voice that came out of her mouth was deep and gravelly and somehow different. It was as if someone else were speaking.

"I have a message from the gods," she said. "A message from the Mother herself. It came to me this morning in the half-light. It came through the fires and the fumes, and it came in blinding strength." Her voice was lower now, but in the silence it seemed as if it could be heard everywhere at once, between the trees and from the sky above.

"There is a curse on you, and on the whole House of Minos!"

The words sank through the air like stones thrown into a lake. Sickness spread out through my body from my stomach. I wanted to retch. Nobody spoke.

My father's face briefly crumpled, then set solid again. There was a deep sadness in his eyes that I had never seen before. It was only there for the smallest moment, but it felt to me as if I had stared into the far reaches of the cosmos, into the places where the gods lived, into somewhere beyond time. He blinked, and the feeling passed.

He stretched out a hand, almost as if he were about to hold Myrrah's.

"Take away that woman," shouted someone. Hunters moved forward uncertainly.

"Wait!" My father's voice rang out imperiously. Everything, and everyone, halted. Time swallowed us all.

"Please, forgive my men," said my father, gently. He motioned to an attendant, who hurried forwards with water. Myrrah pushed away the beaker. She remained, arms held out in front of her, like some figure built to scare away birds. "What is the curse?" asked my father. I could sense the strain in his voice; I hoped that nobody else could.

She pointed her finger at me and at my father.

"There is death in your house, King Minos. There are things twisted out of joint. The stench of darkness is in your minds. And none of you – none of you – will escape it."

A breeze rustled through the trees, and its rushing filled the world.

"I see a confusion full of blood! I see corridors, twisting, turning! Lines filled with blood!" Her voice was loud, ringing, fierce, and an arc of spittle came from her mouth.

"Is there no way out of the curse?" asked my father.

"I see no way out of the curse."

My father, always a king, bowed to her. He offered to have an attendant lead her on a horse to a resting chamber in the palace, but she refused.

No way out? I thought. No way out of the curse?

Myrrah looked at me. Hunters were levelling their weapons; lords were glaring; attendants were panicking. Bansa was poised and ready, his body making an arrow towards me and the woman. Myrrah strode towards me slowly, each step seeming huge.

"In your face I see two things," she muttered. There was a stink on her like smoke and sacrifice.

"What are they?" I asked, trembling, as the noise and shouts and bustle continued around me.

"A monster," she said.

Me? A monster?

"And death."

The word pricked me like the tip of a knife.

Timon approached, more swiftly than his overweight frame seemed capable of. He touched the priestess on the shoulder, and she seemed to grow limp, and clutched at him. He led her away, leaving me standing on my own, the dogs barking around me, my hands slippery with sweat, with a dark taste in my mouth.

I was a thirteen-year-old boy, the son of a king. I had killed a white hind. And I'd been marked by a priestess, for death.

2

BY THE BLACK LAKE

The sun was high in the sky before the white hind, no longer dripping blood, was trussed up on a pole and we were ready to return home. But I was in no mood to celebrate during our silent journey. We came to the Black Lake, the sun reflecting in its still waters. A swan beat down to the surface and glided along. I glanced up miserably – there was the low, wooden house by the side of the water, with a path leading to the front door, and smoke billowing from somewhere inside. I had to speak to her again, the priestess. Was Myrrah prophesying my own death, or somebody close to me? And what did she mean by a monster?

There was a shadow in the doorway, and for a moment I was afraid. Then the shadow detached itself and came forward.

Myrrah's face was barely lined, even though I knew she was older than my father. Her eyes glinted in the sunlight.

She gazed at me. I tried to speak, but I couldn't. Her eyes were holding me. It was as if she could look beneath my skull and find what thoughts lay within. It felt like now there was nothing else in this world, apart from me and Myrrah. I couldn't even feel Swift's hot flanks beneath me.

Timon broke the spell. He brought his horse up beside me. "Greetings, Myrrah," he said.

I snapped back to the moment. "Priestess," I said, bowing my head. "I've come to ask you about the prophecy."

No answer – just that all-seeing gaze. My lips were chapped, and I ran my tongue over them.

"I would like some water. Please will you allow me to rest for a moment in your house?" I spoke formally, not wanting to offend her.

She shifted her body to block the path. I moved Swift forward slightly, and Myrrah held out her arms as if to say: go no further.

Why didn't she want me to go inside the house? What was she hiding in there? She was a priestess, true, but that didn't mean her house was out of bounds.

I tried again, but Myrrah put her hand on Swift, who whinnied and halted.

This was – this was insolence! I looked around, to see if my father, King Minos was in sight. My spear shifted beneath my arm. My mouth felt full of sand.

Myrrah spat, slowly and lazily, on the ground at Swift's feet.

Without thinking, I pulled my sword out of its sheath. Myrrah looked up at me, and for a moment I was poised there, the sword held high, the bright eyes of the priestess tearing into me. The sword felt heavy and I wanted to drop it. I held on to it tightly, not knowing what I was doing. She'd spat at me, and I was thirsty, and I was a prince. Anger was swirling through me, and shame. I wanted to cry.

"Prince!" It was Timon. He'd come up behind me. "May I remind you that the priestess is inviolable?"

I turned to him, and felt Myrrah's gaze shift away. I flicked my tongue over my lips again. My arm dropped. "That does not excuse such behaviour," I managed to whisper. Re-sheathing the sword, I bowed again, curtly.

She just stared ahead, eyes filled with a strange kind of light.

So I sat there, on Swift, feeling ridiculous.

Myrrah delved into the folds of her robe and held out a small flask, which she offered to me. I didn't want to take it. I didn't want Myrrah's water any more. I didn't want anything to do with her. But I still had to know.

"I came to ask you, Myrrah, if you will explain the prophecy to me?"

Her interminable stare. I bowed to her again, cheeks flushing, turned Swift around and left.

I caught up with the King as we neared the palace.

"Father," I said quietly, trying not to draw any attention from Timon, who was sleepily padding along behind us.

He looked at me with a distant gaze. "Mmmm?"

"Myrrah – I went to see her, to ask her about the prophecy. She... she wouldn't let me into her house, and then she spat at the ground in front of me."

"You're trying to tell me that one of the senior priestesses of the Mother Goddess was insolent to you?"

I nodded.

He sighed. "The priestesses cannot be touched, Stephan. They are holy. No doubt Myrrah was simply clearing her throat.

"But—"

"She meant no ill. You must be courteous at all times. To everybody." He kicked his heels into Farseeker, and trotted on.

The palace of Knossos was on the top of a small hill, built out of stone. To me, it looked like it grew out of the ground. Layers of floors rose up into the sky, held up by scarlet pillars. I could see people moving about the terraces, and the guards with their bronze armour flashing.

After taking Swift to her stable, and instructing the stable boys to make sure she had enough food and water in her trough, I made my way round to the stone steps at the front of the main palace complex, the guards at the gate parting to let me through, and went into the darkness of the entrance hall.

I stopped a moment to blink: it was always difficult adjusting your eyes from the light outside. Though there was an opening above, it was cool and gloomy in there.

Somebody barged past me as I came into the dark-ness, and, a little flustered, I turned to see the back of a tall, wiry man, holding several scrolls, walking in the direction of the New Temple. Three or four scribes fol-lowing him all bowed and nodded at me as they went.

"Daedalus!" I called.

The wiry man stopped and turned, spilling a couple of scrolls from his bundle, which were immediately picked up by a scribe, who held them carefully.

"Pulleys," said Daedalus. "Know anything about them?" His eyes were bright.

"Well…" I started to say. "Pulleys…"

"Thought so." Turning, he hurried off to his construc-tion site, where he was building the New Temple to the Mother Goddess. It was to be my father's great legacy: a temple whose beauty and brilliance would be known throughout the Middle Sea, and beyond.

"All will become clear, my prince," he shouted over his shoulder. "The world will marvel at my creation! Now, if you knew anything about steam it might come in handy…" And he turned to one of his scribes, who immediately began jotting something down on a tablet.

Smiling a little, I continued on into the palace. I wanted to see my little brother Asterius, who'd be in his rooms with his nurses. I'd whittled him some wooden toys – a man, a bull and a horse – so I needed to get them from the cedar chest in my bedroom. On the other hand, I also needed to avoid my tutor, Theo – yesterday I'd bunked off my lessons to play on the shore with my sister Ari. So I kept to the busy parts of the palace, where I might go unnoticed, going through the Hall of the Double Axes, past the light well and the workshops and the storerooms, taking the roundabout route.

As I rounded a corner of the kitchens, a wooden stick shot out to bar my way. It was carved with a bull's head, and the horns caught my side.

"Ouch!"

"You may think I am old," murmured Theo, "but I can still work out what you young people are up to…"

"I'm sorry, Theo," I said, and it was partly true. I didn't like making him angry. His lined face in the torchlight looked at me with those sad, wise eyes.

"I'm disappointed in you, Prince," he said. "Your brother Androgeos is such a keen learner, and Ariadne has a quick mind too – quicker than Androgeos's,

I'd say. I still have high hopes for you, but even so – I am instructed by your mother Queen Pasiphaë to confine you to your room as punishment." The way he said it sounded almost apologetic. He never liked punishing me.

"But..." I said, as the kitchen aromas of roasting meat swirled all around me.

"...without supper."

"Theo!" My stomach was empty – I'd hardly eaten all day, nothing but a handful of berries, what with the excitement of the hunt and the weirdness of Myrrah's prophecy.

"It's not for me, or for you, to argue," said Theo.

So off I slunk to my quarters, with Theo walking closely behind. He left me with some exercises to go through (the names of the generals of our armies; the myriad names of the Mother Goddess), and closed the door with a sigh.

A cough as I entered made me look up. My sister, Ari, was leaning against the far wall by the window, looking thoughtful, as she often did. Her long hair – blond, which came from my mother's northern side, though some said she was descended from the sun god – gleamed on her shoulders, matched by a torc around her neck.

"Why aren't you with the men?" she asked.

"Confined to quarters," I said grumpily. "Why are you in my room?" I flopped down onto my couch. I was sweating, and needed to pour cold water over myself. Should I tell her what had happened in the forest?

"Nobody can find me here," she said. "They wouldn't think to look. But listen. I heard something this afternoon. In the market."

"And what were you doing in the market?" It was outside the walls, and Ari had to get permission to go out there – and then go with a full load of attendants. She hated that.

She smiled at me. "That didn't worry you when we went to the beach."

"True," I conceded.

"I have my ways. Nurses fall asleep. Guards don't always know that the girl in the cloak carrying a basket full of eggs is a princess."

"You steal eggs?" I said, only half-joking.

"I put them back." She slid out of the sunlight and drew a fold of material over her face. "See? Now I'm just dozy Dorcas, up for market for the day from a sleepy little village."

"It's dangerous. You could get hurt, or kidnapped."

"Rumours, I heard. Strange rumours."

"What?" She was talking over me. She always did. "All the more reason for you not to go to the market."

My room was cool at that time of day. Ari leant against the wall, back in the light, covering up a frieze of a blue monkey, crinkles appearing on her forehead. She took a breath, choosing her words carefully.

"No, Stephan. All the more reason that I should go. It's important to hear what people are saying."

"And what are they saying?" I slumped back in my couch. "Wait, let me guess." This would be easy if I just conjured up in my mind the petitioners that came to my father daily. "They are unfairly taxed. The gods are against them. The price of corn is too high. There are no siring bulls, and the…"

She blanched, the sun coming off her pale cheeks, her hair as gold as the sunlight, where mine was blacker than the night sky. Like mine, her eyes were light green with a touch of blue.

"They say all that, yes. And they also say that our mother…" She put a slim hand to her throat.

"What about our mother?"

Ari gulped. Her eyelids fluttered up and down. "I… don't know how to say it."

I sat back up, looking at the mixture of confusion, fear and pain in her eyes.

"Please," I said. "Tell me."

Ari nodded. "They say… they say that she and Daedalus…"

"Has he been boring her about pulleys and steam?" I said, searching for a joke to ward off a dismal feeling, thinking of those bright, shadowed eyes.

"Daedalus… and my mother…" Ari was trembling. "They say they are lovers."

"But that's ridiculous!" I cut in, almost giddy with relief that the terrible rumour was so stupid.

"It is, isn't it?" she pleaded.

My mother, and Daedalus? I'd never even seen them together, never mind known them to pass a word. How could they meet, when she was married to my father, King Minos, and Daedalus was forever buried among his drawings and his beloved building works? A quiet rage came over me. "Gossip, that's all it is. She mustn't hear of this."

"No. Absolutely not," Ari answered, as I sunk my head in my hands – first Myrrah and her horrible prophecy, now idiots spreading insulting rumours. "But what's the matter, Stephan? If it's no more than a rumour?"

I clenched my hands together. Should I tell her about the prophecy, about Myrrah?

Ari always knew what to do, how to get what she wanted. She started to poke me playfully, drawing a smile from me despite myself. And then I said, "Ari. Something awful happened today."

The white hind and the prophecy, Myrrah's wicked presence at the Black Lake, the spittle of the silent priestess on the ground near my feet – after I'd gone through the whole thing, Ari brooded, taking her time to answer.

"Interesting. You say she barred your way?"

I nodded. "She wouldn't let me go down the path. And more – Swift didn't seem to want to go either. Swift sensed something, I think."

"And there was smoke coming from the house?"

"There was." Suddenly I realized how odd that was. A blazing fire, in the heat of summer?

"Stephan," said Ari carefully, her eyes serious but bright, "let's go down to the Black Lake, and see what Myrrah's doing. Why would she behave like that? Isn't it treasonous?"

"How shall we go?" I asked. "You don't have the excuses I have to leave the palace, and I find it hard enough to get away from Theo."

Ari folded her cloak over her head again. "Eggs, eggs, fresh-laid eggs!"

"You can't pull that one again."

"I always have a way."

And it was true, she always did have a way. Ari knew the palace complex much better than I did, always slipping in and out of places, like a cat. As quick as smoke, Theo used to say.

"We can't tell anyone," I said, remembering my father the King, and how he'd reacted when I'd told him.

"Night is our friend," said Ari. "Be ready for me." She stood up – and then she was gone, as fast as a dragonfly slips from the surface of a stream.

3

THE REEK OF DEATH

Later that night, my bodyservant Bansa came in to attend me as I went to bed. He was wearing a new belt, into which he'd stuck a short dagger.

"Got it from the market today!" he said. "Look! I'm Perseus killing the sea dragon!" he shouted, stabbing the air a few times. "Take that, slimy beast! And that! Hah!"

I put down the list of generals I'd been learning, which had turned into meaningless sounds in my head.

"What else did you get?" I asked, hopefully, thinking about food, as Bansa finished with his imaginary beast and pretended to release Andromeda from her chains.

"Saw a few things, bought a few things," he said, flopping down on the couch. "Lots of people. Man from Egypt selling potions! Not sure if he was really from Egypt though – he didn't sound like it… And there was a woman up from the village selling goat's cheese: she let me have a bit for free… Delicious!"

My stomach rumbled.

"Got you some food too," he said in a small voice, taking out some olives and bread from his pouch and a small bit of goat's cheese. I laughed as I thanked him, and he did an impression of a dog.

"I'm tired, Bansa," I said, after I'd eaten, and held out my tunic, which he took with a pained expression, putting it away in the cedar chest.

When he had gone to his bed in my antechamber, I sat awake by the light of a small flaming torch. I was annoyed that I hadn't been able to see Aster to give him his toys. For safekeeping I put them in the pouch I always wore around my waist – he could have them in the morning. But now I needed to be ready for Ari's arrival.

I put my hunting tunic back on, and girded my waist with a short sword. Then there was nothing to do but wait. I couldn't concentrate on anything very much, and tapped my foot restlessly.

Towards the middle of the night – I could tell by the position of the moon, which sailed across my high window – came a soft sound at my door.

Ari put her finger to her lips, and we tiptoed past the small, slightly snoring bundle that was Bansa, out into the corridor. She thrust a cloak at me. Under hers she was wearing a man's tunic she must have taken from somewhere. It fitted her very well. "Wear this," she whispered. "If we see anyone, we hide; if we can't hide, we cover our faces and pretend to be… you know." She mimed someone kissing. I raised an eyebrow, but followed, unquestioning. "Come on," she continued. "I know a way out."

"Unguarded?"

"You'll see."

Those echoing corridors, lit by torches that coughed and wheezed like the old men of my father's council, seemed to look down on us with baleful eyes. Once we heard the clank of bronze, a sword hitting a shield as the guard walked, and we hid, hardly breathing, behind a long tapestry that showed the Mother Goddess making the world.

When the guard had gone, emboldened, I almost overtook Ari, but she waved me back. We reached a warren of passages that intertwined behind the Great Hall, where our father would sit in state. I didn't know exactly where we were – these were the endless rooms containing archives, tablets, all the dry lists that did not interest me at all – records of laundry, olives, goats, salaries, fines, all the things that men and women did in the palace, and that Timon, the steward, controlled.

Ari flattened herself against the wall, breathing deeply, and I quickly followed her into the shadows. Timon, muttering, lit by flame, appeared at the end of the passageway in which we stood. He was with someone I did not recognize – not that that was uncommon, in the palace. Who knew how many people lived in the complex? Like ants in a nest, I sometimes thought.

"The letter was received by the King himself?" Timon was saying.

A mumble by way of reply, which I couldn't make out. "And you're sure it went into the hand of the King? That nobody else read it?"

This time the reply was clearer. "I put it there myself, and he read it in front of me, and then he burned it. Nobody else was there."

"Then it is for Aegeus to decide now," said Timon.

Aegeus? Why was Timon talking about King Aegeus of Athens? We had an uneasy pact with his kingdom, and my brother Andro was in Athens on embassy, seeking an alliance over trade routes through the Middle Sea, from the shores of Africa to Asia in the east, which we controlled; it must have something to do with that. But then why meet here, in the dark, in an obscure corner of the palace? We had designs on Athens, I knew, but what sort of secret plot was Timon involved in?

Timon chose that moment to move, and Ari, impatient, pulled at my sleeve and led me onwards. She took me further into that wing of the palace, which I guessed was eastwards, than I had ever been before. The smells of cheeses filled my nostrils; we must have been going past storerooms. My stomach rumbled, and Ari looked back at me and frowned mockingly.

We came out into a courtyard. The tree that stood in a corner crouched like a sinister giant. It was easy to believe a spirit might inhabit it.

"Follow me," said Ari, and skittered fearlessly over to the tree. Without looking back, she disappeared up the trunk as fast as a lizard. Quickly glancing around to see that we were not observed, I followed, hauling myself up behind her.

There was a deep drop on the other side; I jumped down, falling on all fours, and joined Ari, who was waiting for me. The moon cast a clear light over the path, and gleamed off her blond hair, so she slipped into the shadows. She'd taken off her torc, but her neck shone whitely.

Ari seemed to know exactly where she was going – how many times had she sneaked out before at night, I wondered? An owl hooted low and swept above our heads. An omen? I didn't know what the owl might mean, but I didn't like the thought of it.

As we entered the forest, haunt of wild boar and bears and maybe worse, I was glad to feel my short sword in its sheath by my side. Andro had written to us about a huge bull near Marathon, just north-east of the city, which ravaged the countryside around it, ate men and trampled all in its path.

I shivered, thinking about this and other, stranger things in the stories we were told. Andro singing about night and chaos. The People of the Mountains. The darker shadow gods, who tricked humans, who brought disease and death.

Ari pressed on through the woods unafraid, with me at her heels like a shadow. Suddenly she pushed me back against a tree and gestured with her elbow. I followed the line, hoping it was nothing that had teeth and claws, frightened that it might be something from the blacker parts of the world.

There, standing at the rushing brook, calm in the moonlight, was a woman. She was tall, and her head was bowed down, almost like a swan's curving neck. She was wearing some kind of cloth, but it rippled and shone strangely. She bent down and kissed the surface of the water, and light came from her and spread either way. I held my breath.

We waited while she stood, looking upstream; and then she stepped into the shallows, and waded upwards. We stood there, as still as we could, until it seemed as if she'd merged with the water.

"One of the mountain people," whispered Ari in the silence.

The light grew faint, and dimmed. I let out my breath. A truly holy sight – this what we had witnessed.

Ari pulled something from her belt and, after a few false starts, lit a small torch.

"You think of everything," I said. In the moonlight, the torch flames on her face, her expression didn't change. Her mouth was set.

The journey was easy. The stream ran by us, glistening, cool and inviting, its chattering underpinning the deeper rustlings of the forest. The moon hadn't risen much higher when we reached the low house where Myrrah lived.

No fire was burning now, and not a light shone. I could feel the cold expanse of the lake to my right, and the breeze on my skin. Ari extinguished the torch, and the world was all silver.

"Now what?" I whispered, half-mocking.

She edged round the clearing, and I followed, approaching the wooden building from the back. It was a simple place, built originally for a hunting lodge. "There aren't many rooms," she said, in low tones. "We'll look in through the back. We might be able to see what she's hiding in there."

The back of the house had a wooden door with windows on either side. Dashing across to it like she was made of darkness, Ari slid her hand into a gap and made a quick jiggling movement, then held up her other hand to stop the door from creaking open. The light wind rustled my hair; and before I knew it, she was through. And I, afraid of what might be outside in the night, and of her disapproval, followed.

It was dim inside the house, with a faint glow coming from a door further up the corridor. The floor beneath my feet was strewn with something like grasses, softening our footfalls. In the air was the faint tang of some sort of stew. One of the doors was slightly open: from it came the lowest of mutterings. Tiptoeing past it, we peered in.

Inside, lit by low torchlight, Myrrah was kneeling in front of an altar. She was chanting so quietly I could not make out the words – unless she was speaking a tongue beyond my knowledge. Smoke from a torch by the entrance seeped out. I stifled a cough.

It was good that she was praying, so she wouldn't be distracted by our noise. I don't know why, but I wondered whom she was praying to – the Mother Goddess? Or some other being? I didn't want to find out.

Ari pointed up a short flight of stairs; we climbed it carefully, twitching at every creak. Something was knocking at my mind, telling me that we were not wanted.

The hallway upstairs was narrow, with only three doors off it that I could see. Moonlight came through a small, open window. Ari tried the first door, and opened it. I crowded in behind her. There was an empty space, with a low couch in it, and nothing else.

I jiggled the handle of the second. Inside, a bat flittered away, and I jumped back, only just managing not to cry out.

We went to the third. Only later, much later, did I recall that an owl hooted once more. Impatient, Ari eased it open. I couldn't see anything. Then Ari pushed the door wide open.

The stench hit me first. Slowly, my eyes allowed what my mind could not have imagined.

I do not think I have ever seen such things, even at the hunt. My stomach sickened, and I felt Ari tense beside me and put a hand to her mouth. She bent over, holding the door post. I gripped my dagger's handle.

The severed heads, the dismembered bodies, of animals, ghastly pale in the moonlight – a bear, the destroyed carcass of a deer, even a foal, on its back, its guts pulled out. There was some kind of great lizard, and beasts I did not recognize, and around it all the buzzing of myriad flies.

The images of the slaughtered animals came in and out of the darkness, lit by the shimmering torch and the moon, as though they still had some kind of horrible life.

"We should go," I whispered, barely able to contain myself. What was Myrrah doing in this place? All this slaughter?

It was too much: the stench, those staring eyes.

Ari grabbed my arm and we rushed out, hands over our nostrils, tumbling down the stairs, not caring about disturbing Myrrah. We ran into the forest, and I turned as we entered and looked back briefly. There, framed in the doorway and carrying a torch, was Myrrah. Her eyes glittered. She was lofty, and she held her hand up – to bless us, or to curse us.

We ran, as fast as we could, blindly through the forest, under the cold light of the moon goddess, our legs whipped by branches, stumbling and panting.

When we returned to the palace, we crept back, chastened, to our separate quarters. So many questions tumbled in my brain, like acrobats, only with no order, nothing. Did our parents know about this? Did anyone know about this? The slaughter of animals, the reek of death, the priestess's knowing prophecies?

As I shuddered into sleep, the stench of those rotting corpses kept returning to me, and Myrrah's face, illuminated by the torch, sinister and calm.

4

Betrayal in Athens

I woke the next morning to Bansa tugging at my shoulder.

"Get up, prince! Prince!"

"What's going on, Bansa?" I said.

Bansa sat on the end of my bed and put a hand over his face. "Guards say they saw an exhausted soldier running up the avenue, bearing a royal letter. They've taken him in and woken up the King and Queen. Came to get you because I knew they'd want you." He made a half-hearted attempt at a bow.

Outside in the passages there were people rushing about: soldiers in bronze holding torches that flickered in the dark; groups of maids, who kept their eyes downcast as they passed me and poked each other and giggled when they thought I wasn't looking; men and women on their own, walking purposefully, with set looks on their faces.

I ran into Ari coming from her quarters.

"I hope it's nothing bad," she said – but she hardly sounded convinced. "Let's pray," I replied, trying to keep my mind on the Mother Goddess as we approached the Small Chamber.

Within, standing on the mosaic of gold and blue stones with its pattern of lilies, Timon was waiting, encased in a red tunic embroidered with gold monkeys. He raised a painted eyebrow as we entered, and put his hands together. They gleamed with rings.

My father and mother were seated on draped wooden chairs behind the high table, gilded with red and purple. A stone jug of wine stood by them, but I could see it was untouched. The Small Chamber was an inner chamber, cool and dark, that came off my father's private rooms. This room was where intimate family business was decided – missions for Andro, nurses for Aster, suitors for Ari – and soon, possible brides for me (none yet, as I frequently thanked the gods, though there had been noises about Glauce, the King of Corinth's daughter, who was a good few years older than me.)

My little brother Aster was sitting by the side on a stool, clutching his nurse's hand. He moaned – even he could tell something bad was happening. I went over to him and stroked his head, and from my pouch gave him the little wooden toys I'd made. He rocked back and forth, and set them out on the ground.

My father, King Minos, was in an official purple robe, and my mother was clasping his arm. I rarely saw them touching in public. I could see that both of them were suppressing some deep emotion, as we were always taught to do. Dread at what had brought us all here clamped at my guts.

Timon closed the door. "My king," he said.

"I will tell my own children," said my father. "The royal children." Aster made a sound that could have been a laugh. His nurse shushed him.

My mother nodded. "Yes, Timon. You may leave us."

Timon bowed, slowly, perspiration trickling down his forehead. He paused at the door, as if to say something, but instead bowed again and left.

Ari and I ran to our parents. My father's cheek was twitching. "There is news from Athens," he said.

"What is it?" I asked in the pause that followed.

My mother drew herself up and cleared her throat. "Androgeos," she said. "Your brother. My son, and the heir to Crete." She placed a hand on mine, and another on Ari's. "He has… died."

And suddenly she wept, her tears dropping to the table. Aster was rocking back and forth. Did he know? Could he tell what had happened? There was a blackness inside me, as Andro's image came to me, a moment from when I was little. We were playing down by the stream: he was a general, and I was a soldier, and he was ordering me about. He was always ordering me about. It was hot, I remember, the sun burning my neck. He told me to jump over a gate which rose tall against the sky. I paced up to it; leapt; and I fell to the ground, my arms and legs grazed, a bump on my head swelling up to the size of an egg.

Andro didn't laugh: instead he ran towards me, picked me up, soothed me; he carried me all the way back to the palace, and stayed with me while the nurses pressed leaves to my wounds and told me a story about a queen made from ice, and a boy she enchanted, and the girl who went to find him. Andro had been so far away from me, most of our lives – but even so, I felt the pain of his loss like a burn.

I felt tears rise. I glanced at Ari, and saw that she too was brushing them away.

"The messenger came early this morning," said my father. The dim light made everything dreamlike and slow.

"How does he know – the messenger?" This was Ari, fingering her finely worked golden bracelets, trying to suppress her sadness. Aster had run to her, and she was holding him gently. Ari, above all, loved Andro.

I loved him too – though, I confess, now something was lurking in the background of my mind, an eagle's shadow hovering over a hare: what did this catastrophe mean for me?

"He has Andro's token." King Minos put it on the table between us: the ring of the House of the Double Axe, worn by the heir to the kingdom, burnished gold and heavy. I said, "We must talk to the messenger."

My father nodded, and sighed. The weight of things was pressing on him.

"I'll send for him," I said. I kissed my father's hand, then, glancing at Ari, opened the door where Bansa and Timon were skulking. Bansa was unusually quiet, twisting one foot around his other leg and poking at a

43

hole in the wall; Timon was standing with his hands folded. Nodding to Timon, I sent Bansa to fetch the messenger. He seemed relieved to follow my instructions, and I returned into the private chamber.

I thought I could see the traces of tears on my father's face. My mother's still flowed, though she maintained her composure.

Nobody spoke. All that could be heard were the clicking sounds of Aster moving his little toys up and down on the stone floor.

The door opened after a while, and Timon let the messenger in; I pointedly waited until Timon had left before shutting it again.

The messenger was covered in poultices and limping, his face ashen, and he smelt rank, of sweat and blood.

Despite his condition, he bowed low to my parents, and then to us. My mother greeted him formally, and ordered food, drink and a chair to be brought for him; while he was settling, I watched him. He had a beaker of something hot given to him, and a plate of cold meats and herby breads and olives and grapes was set by his side.

"My king," he croaked when all the servants had gone. "My queen. And Prince Stephanos, and Princess Ariadne."

"I remember you," I said. "You're Lysias, Lord Nicodemus's son. You served my brother – since he was young."

"True," he said, not curtly, but with the directness of a soldier.

"But we haven't seen you for a year. How do we know you are who you say you are?" This was my father, ever careful.

"You have his token," said the man. "He gave it to me himself. I can tell you what happened. If you still don't believe me, my father is here in the court: he will vouch that I am Lysias." He coughed, for a long time. The flames in their brackets flickered. "My king… This is all I can tell you, all that I saw." He looked down at the ground.

"Continue," said my father.

"Aegeus has a son, Theseus – who is a couple of years older than you, Prince, and as excellent a fighter as anyone's seen."

I blushed at the implied comparison, and covered up my embarrassment with a brisk sip of wine.

"So our days would pass, in feasting, boasting and play. Androgeos was doing your father great service, and he was a firm favourite of King Aegeus. Then, one day, a change came over Aegeus. He was not so hearty at his meals, and he didn't ask Androgeos to sing. Do you remember what a fine voice he had?"

I did. I remembered his singing of the drifting moon and the toiling sun, of rain and fire and how the world began. It was a talent my father discouraged – what prince sings like a common bard, after all? – but he would do it, sometimes, for us, as we sat together in our parents' chambers.

"One of the bards was singing, after the feast, about a hero who had slain a monstrous boar – Meleager, the son of the King of Calydon. The hall was silent when he ended – he sang so beautifully. Almost as soon as he'd finished, a man came rushing in – a petitioner, from a region nearby, who told us how the ravages of the Marathonian bull grew greater every day."

My mother shuddered.

"Theseus, drunk, sprang up and vowed to slay it, but Aegeus forbade it. All eyes turned to Androgeos. He stood up slowly, more assured than the puppyish

46

Athenian prince. 'I will kill the beast,' he exclaimed. 'And I will bring safety to Athens and honour to Crete.' The hall roared – this would cement our alliance, I thought.

"And so we set off, after a day's preparations, with the petitioner as a guide. Theseus watched us go. I saw him and Androgeos clasping hands. He seems a sweet prince, and I hope he had nothing to do with what came next." Lysias paused and bit off a chunk of bread and meat which he'd taken from his plate. "Forgive me, but I have come a long way, and in great danger too."

We waited until he'd swallowed his meat and followed it up with huge gulps of hot wine.

"The first day we laughed and joked. We had an escort of soldiers from Aegeus. We scoffed at the stories that came our way – the bull's neck was thicker than an oak's trunk; its eyes spat fires. We camped for the night by a stream. The day was long and hot, and we were weary. The soldiers offered us wine; I refused. They pressed it on me, so I took a mouthful, but spat it out when they weren't looking. I wanted to clear my head. And lucky that I did so.

"I didn't sleep well. Rumours may be rumours, but in the dark, in an unknown place, they take on greater terror. I was awake, my eyes half open, praying to the Mother Goddess, when I heard one of the Athenian men give a low whistle. I was on the alert immediately.

"At once the Athenian traitors all sprang up. The first of our men they stabbed didn't even cry out. I heard the squelch of his body and wondered why nobody else was woken.

"They must have drugged our soldiers, I realized. When I saw them approach Androgeos, I sprang up with my sword and leapt at them. Because I'd taken them by surprise I managed to kill a few – but there were too many of them, and they had the advantage. I slashed at one of them just as I heard a cry.

"It was Androgeos. He'd woken up, as they stuck a sword into him. He caught my eyes in the light of the campfire. 'Run!' he gasped. He slipped the ring off his finger and threw it to me. It fell by my foot – I picked it up. I understood. I looked around me – my horse was within reach. I could make it – I hacked into another soldier.

"'So much for your prince,' shouted one of them. 'Aegeus will have his way now.'

"I'd reached my horse. I leapt onto her back. I'm sorry to say that I... I injured the other horses so that they couldn't follow me."

He looked ashamed, and I thought of my own horse, Swift, and how I could never hurt her.

"Then I sliced through the rope tying mine to a tree, and spurred her on. They chased me, but my horse was too fast, theirs too hurt. And in the next village I disguised myself, found a way to the sea. I hid myself from sight, and found a Cretan trader who gave me passage. This was the day before yesterday. I returned to Knossos this morning."

The wall tapestries hung still, telling the same stories for ever; the torchlight flickered. My father clenched his hands. My mother's were at her temples. Ari had gone white. Treachery! The treachery of the Athenians. How could they have treated my brother in this way?

"He should have died a hero's death," I said. A hot fury I'd never felt before bubbled inside me, came out through my mouth. "We should attack them, at once – to avenge him!"

If there were ever words I came to regret later, it was these. They say that everything is connected, like a great thread, closely linked. I wish I could unpick this one from the tapestry. But my words were in the air like stones flung from a sling.

Ari said, "Shouldn't we try to parley? They could pay blood ransom."

"For the heir to my kingdom," said Minos, "there would not be enough ransom in all Athens." He looked at me. I knew what was coming. The eagle's shadow was above me. I could tell Minos's words before he said them.

"You are the heir now." He'd said it – and he gave me the ring. The thing that had been looming in my mind became solid, like a phantom that gibbers by your bedside and is still there when you wake, when your mouth goes dry from trying to scream.

So Crete would be mine – the palace, the kingdom, the empire. When Minos died, I would be the King of Crete.

I did not like that thought at all.

I toyed with the ring, then placed it on my finger. It felt as if I was betraying Andro.

"It's too big," I said, showing how easily it slipped off. I gave it back to my father, and choked down a sob.

"We will have it changed." He gazed at me, his eyes tender. I could feel that he wanted to say something more. "You are the heir now," he said again, as if that was enough. I felt his expectation on me like a physical thing. This shouldn't have happened. Andro was going to be king, not me. What did I know about being a king?

My mother's tears were greater now. I released the sob I'd been holding in. My mother set up a lament, and Ari joined. My father watched them, and the light glinted off his eyes.

"We must bury Androgeos properly," he said. "The People of the Mountains…"

There was an old story about the People of the Mountains, which told how, at the death of the heir to Crete, they would stand at the funeral pyre and bring gifts to the new heir. A story lost in the past, that my nurse had told me. They'd come for Minos, and brought him a bronze statue, called Talos, that sat in the Great Hall as a symbol of justice. The people said that it moved at night; even that it paced the shoreline of the island; but I'd never seen it even twitch.

Minos gathered himself:

"I think the time has come for Athens to feel our strength." He stood up, towering and magnificent now in that room. "Call the council. At once." He swept out to the sounds of keening, a father and a king.

Lysias drained his beaker, and coughed once more. He waited for my mother's sobbings to still; it seemed an age before she stopped.

"There is one thing I have left to tell," he said.

"What's that, Lysias?" My mother recovered herself. She would perform the ritual mourning later – the tearing of the hair, the rending of clothes, the raking of cheeks with her nails, and Ari would do it as well, and I would watch, while nursing revenge in my heart.

"That morning, the morning we set out," he said. "I saw a messenger come to the palace of Aegeus. That wasn't so special. Only…" he sighed.

"Only what?" said Ari.

"He was wearing Cretan clothes."

The implications buzzed around my brain. Had someone from our palace betrayed Andro? Was somebody working with King Aegeus?

Something was at work in the palace, and I didn't like it. I remembered Timon in the corridors at midnight, and the letter he'd sent. I wanted to go and think it over, and took leave from my mother and Ari.

In the passageway I stumbled across a small group of kitchen maids giggling:

"I wonder how big his horns are now."

"Do you think they're showing? Are they on his forehead or on the sides of his head?"

"Or somewhere else…" sniggered another.

What were those girls gossiping about? They scattered when they saw me. Ignoring them, I gripped my sword handle and went looking for my father, King Minos.

5

The Curse Begins

I was filled with fury, fuelled by grief. We had been betrayed – and it looked like someone inside the palace was involved. Could it be Timon? What could his motives be? There might be others in the palace who were plotting.

The councillors were already assembled in the council chamber adjoining the Great Hall of the Double Axes – smaller than the Hall, yet with space for everyone to sit on benches. There were tables laid with jugs of wine, plates of glistening olives and dates and bowls of honey and freshly cooked bread. I hadn't eaten yet that day, and my stomach rumbled. My throat was parched, and I nodded to Bansa, who sloped off and brought me back a goblet. I sipped from it greedily.

My father was speaking above the noise of the councillors. Tall windows on either side of the room lit up the whole space with daylight. I looked at the frieze behind the throne, which showed the Mother Goddess, in all her aspects, and below her the grim faces of the shadow gods.

"Attack them immediately! Bring them to heel!" someone cried, to shouts of agreement.

"Send an embassy first!" came a louder voice.

"So that they can be slaughtered too?" My father noticed me, and I went to stand by his chair. "What do you think, Prince Deucalion Stephanos?"

The room went silent but for a few wheezes and coughs from the more ancient of the councillors. Above, a bird fluttered from one window to the other, cooing as it went. A wood pigeon, trapped.

Timon was standing in the far right-hand corner, by the door. There were also Lysias's father, Lord Nicodemus, and six or seven others, including Bansa's father, Lord Callias, a lofty man who usually had a smile just like his son's. Not today.

My mother and Ari entered; the councillors quietened and made way for them. They came to stand with me and my father, Ari to my left, my mother Pasiphaë on my father's right. The livid marks on my mother and Ari's cheeks showed how they'd raked them with their nails, and it made me shudder.

What *did* I think? The councillors' expectation weighed on me. Now I had to show myself as a true leader. Andro would have done it. I had to be decisive – for him.

Gulping a little, turning it into a cough to hide my nervousness, I said, "If Androgeos was murdered by Aegeus, on his direct orders, it is a slight to our honour. And our honour must be restored."

Most of the men in the chamber cheered, even Timon, who clapped his hands together.

"So we should embark with a force to their port of Piraeus, and when we land, we should send an embassy immediately to Aegeus. If he explains himself, we can come to an agreement about a blood ransom. If not – then we attack. We have greater forces than he does."

"A fine answer," said my father, rapping his staff on the ground. The beating sound startled the wood pigeon, which flapped off through the window. There were more noises of approval from the councillors. Lysias's father, shaking his head, was turning to talk to Bansa's. I looked at Ari, who nodded at me. She resembled Andro so strongly that I had to blink a few times to dispel the image.

Lysias's father, Lord Nicodemus, spoke. "We don't need an embassy! We should bring them to heel! Attack at once, no warning, nothing. I'll send Lysias in the vanguard. I'd fight, but I'm too old now. We should attack, destroy, show no mercy."

Bansa's father ruffled his cloak, which he always wore, despite the warmth. He stroked his cheeks, his pale eyes staring. "I urge caution, my king," he said. "We should wait for news from Athens – our armies are scattered, and it will take time to bring them together."

"We have forces enough on the peninsula, garrisoning our colonies," said Lysias's father gruffly.

Lord Nicodemus growled, glaring at me; Lord Callias's gentle voice tried to make compromises. The arguments raged, but I had said all I needed to say, and all I could think now is that it had been the death of my brother that had brought me here, standing where he should be standing.

Eventually, my father, King Minos, raised his sceptre and commanded, in a voice that rolled around the room, "So be it. As my son Deucalion Stephanos suggested, we shall send a messenger to the Cretan force in the peninsula, and also to our cohorts elsewhere. We ourselves shall go at the head of an embassy to parley with the Athenian king, the murderer Aegeus. If we are not successful, we shall attack." He looked at me and bowed his head slightly. My mother, distracted, was staring blankly at the hangings on the walls. Ari hugged herself miserably.

And me – I was filled with pride. I wanted to show myself worthy of my father and of Andro. I imagined myself fighting, hand to hand, with Theseus, and winning, and being held aloft whilst all the soldiers around me called my name.

"And who will rule in your stead?" This was Timon, speaking loudly from his position at the back.

"Queen Pasiphaë, our wife, and Prince Deucalion Stephanos, our son, will be joint regent while we are gone."

What? I turned sharply. I was being made regent? That wasn't fair. Why couldn't Ari do it? She was older than me and knew more about the palace. But my father's warning glance stopped me from shouting out in frustration.

Well, I thought, if I couldn't avenge Andro directly, at least I could honour him here – his gentle voice, which sat so strangely with his soldierly character, his proud soul. And if I were going to be regent, then at least I might be able to find out what was really going on inside the palace – and Ari would help me too. All this double-crossing and plotting was something I'd have to get to grips with. A sudden rush of admiration for my father descended on me. How many plots against his life might there have been?

My father called the council meeting to an end, and the general assembly broke out into clusters, like the sea growing stormy.

Now the army would have to be brought together, and plans drawn up, quickly, and armour made, and supplies seen to. I would have to be kept informed of everything, as would my mother, Pasiphaë.

Theo, my tutor, hobbling his way over to me, grabbed my arm. Inside I cursed – this was no time for upbraiding a truant.

He was practically beaming, showing his teeth, the colour of curdling milk.

"Young prince," he said. "Or should I say regent?"

"Not quite yet, Theo," I said.

"I must instruct you immediately in the ways of kingship. Now you are regent – and, more importantly, the heir…"

I let his quavery voice drift over me, like sacrificial smoke in the wind, and watched the councillors as they milled and chattered. Timon seemed to be firmly situated in a group of men that included Lords Nicodemus and Callias, so I called Bansa over from his perch and whispered to him to keep an eye on Timon. He nodded, his little head bobbing up and down, and flitted away. If anyone could look innocent, it was Bansa.

"Virtue… duty to the Mother Goddess…" Theo was babbling on, "the body of Crete is your body… honour…" His grip, despite his age, was like a bear's teeth in its prey. Ari, watching nearby, read my mind – I knew she'd try to free me from his clutches.

"Did you attend the hunt, Theo?" she asked, sidling up to him.

"I am too old," he said wistfully. "Too, too old. Why, I remember the days when you young ones respected your elders!" He resettled his grip on my arm. "And now this… it's grave, very grave. There will be a war, I have no doubt about it."

"A victory for Crete," I said, mostly because I felt I had to say something.

"But your regency is what we should be talking about. It brings to mind a precedent, from the court of King... ah, was it Pandoricus?"

Ari caught my eye and, despite all that had happened, we managed to exchange the smallest of smiles. She was leading him astray, and soon I'd be free of him.

"Pandoricus, of course," said Ari. "He was the king who had a pet donkey, wasn't he? And didn't he make the donkey a councillor?"

"Why, er, I'm, er, not quite sure about that, Ariadne," said Theo. "Now, if you remember—"

The doors to the Chamber creaked open, and a hush enveloped the room. I turned to see a dark figure standing in the doorway, arms outstretched. Theo mumbled something under his breath, his grip loosening on my arm. The guards around the edges of the room shifted their stances, unsure.

"The curse begins!" It was Myrrah, robed in white, her hair uncoiled. She was filthy, stinking, mud-spattered. "The curse begins! It has taken Androgeos in its grasp..."

Minos blanched. "Priestess…" he said. "How can we avert it?"

Myrrah swept her gaze around the room, her burning eyes taking in everyone and everything. My whole body shivered.

"Sanctuary!" she cried. Her face was frozen, and the voice that came out of her mouth was deep. It wasn't her voice. "For sanctuary, for purification, you must bring me one of your own."

"What do you mean, priestess?" said Minos.

The councillors were jostling, unsure; in my chest my heart was pounding.

"The youngest," said Myrrah, in that rough, deep voice. "Bring me the youngest. Bring me Prince Asterius!"

"Explain yourself, priestess." It was Minos, his voice controlled and courteous. Could she mean death? I wondered. I wouldn't put it past her.

The councillors made way for her, Lords Nicodemus and Callias bowing slightly to her as she swished past. Timon scuttled forward from somewhere.

Myrrah rustled to a stop just by my father. She spoke, again in that deep, scratchy voice. "I must take Prince

Asterius into my safe-keeping, to protect him from harm."

I felt relief, of a sort. He would be safe – but with Myrrah?

Pity and tenderness rushed over Minos's face, so quickly that nobody else would have noticed.

"Priestess," he said, "if you will come with me into a private chamber, we can discuss it there."

Myrrah bowed. I tried to catch up with my father, but he said, "No, Stephan."

Disappointed, I watched Minos disappear through a small door with the priestess. As soon as he'd gone, the councillors began talking, and I made my way over to Ari.

"Watch him," said Ari. "Watch Aster. I don't like this at all."

6

A MESSAGE FROM THE MOUNTAINS

Aster had seemed all right, at first. I'd held him when he was born – a tiny, pink scrap with a raw wail that shredded the air. I was only three, but I can see it as if it were yesterday. He was sickly, and when you dangled things in front of his eyes it was like he was looking somewhere else. They hoped he was blessed by the gods – thought he might even be a seer.

But he stayed like that – looking into the gaps between things, or maybe just into his own mind. He didn't learn how to talk. Instead he made only a kind of low, moaning noise, like a cow. Something was wrong in his mind, and there was nothing anyone could do about it.

We took him to the temple of the Mother Goddess for a blessing, to see what the auguries were – our people found our destinies in the guts of animals, in the flight of birds, in the moanings of inspired priestesses.

The high priestess of the Mother Goddess, standing so high up, so high that in my mind she touched the roof of the temple. White-robed, she was thickset, and her long nose looked even longer when I saw the shadow of it on the wall. Her eyes were calm. I remember her smiling sadly.

The friezes in the temple showed the silver double axe, and the golden bull's horns. The priest – a young, firm man, with brown hair slicked to his head – put on the ritual mask of a bull, then held down a cockerel on the altar. A jet of blood; he bent over the bird like I'd seen farmers tending to their sick lambs. A lock fell over his forehead, which he let stay there. The blood, pooling in rivulets, collecting into patterns, seeped into the earth.

I saw him grimace when he thought my mother wasn't looking – but I was sitting just behind him, kicking my legs against the stone, and I could see that the inside of the cockerel he'd slain was rotting. The priestess looked into the guts, and her brow crinkled.

Aster was damaged – that's what it meant. I remember being taken away, put to bed, told to forget all about it.

But how could I forget?

Saying goodbye to Ari, I decided to stay in my room, so that if anything happened in Aster's chambers, which were near to mine, I would know about it.

Towards the middle of the night, I could hear Aster muttering in the passageway. I looked through the crack in the door – so small, he was, for his ten years, staggering and confused. A helmeted guard stood on each side of him, one gently holding his shoulder, as one of his nurses, Mina, scurried behind. This was it. They were taking him away to Myrrah. My mother was at the head of the melancholy procession. Though she was wrapped in a long dark cloak, with a veil covering her face, I could see the sign of our house on a ring on her finger. The double-headed axe.

Aster moaned louder, and my mother turned to him and placed a hand on his head. The guards' swords gleamed in the torchlight, reflecting from the bright colours of the friezes. That look in Aster's eyes – he walked straight past me, so close.

I waited till they had gone round the corner, edged out of the room and followed softly after them in my bare feet, paddling through the patches of light from the smoky torches on the brackets.

They kept to the family quarters in the southern side of the compound: a series of cool colonnades, with large rooms leading off them, and small squares with tree-shaded fountains and places to sit. We passed nobody. Eventually they came to a door in the south-western corner of the outer wall, leading on to a small courtyard where women brought in water from a well that stood outside. Beyond that was a path down to the woods.

My mother took out a large key from some fold in her robe and opened the lock, and went through, looking neither left nor right. My brother followed, and the guards went after him.

A few seconds later I leapt across the small space and gazed out into the night, trying to keep as far out of the frame of the door as possible.

Low voices, the flash of a flaming torch, the shifting of a horse's hooves and the chink of its bridle... Then a sudden loud moan, which must have been my brother; and then a horse snorting, teeth clicking. The horse was setting off.

I slid to the right, in the opposite direction from which we'd come, as my mother, still shrouded, returned with the guards and the nurse in her wake. As my mother stopped on the threshold she dropped to her knees and kissed the ground, and bowed, three times, touching her forehead to the floor, as we do before the statue of the Mother Goddess. The guards offered to help her up, but she refused.

There was no sign of Aster. My mother locked the door, and the four swept back the way they'd come, the guards a few paces behind my mother, the light they bore throwing spidery shadows on the walls, Mina the nurse behind them, her hands held tightly together. When they'd gone, I peered through the keyhole; but could see nothing, hear nothing, except for the cool wind in the cypresses.

I walked slowly back to my chamber, where Bansa lay still as a stone, and sat on the window ledge, gazing out into the darkness, watching the trees in the moonlight. I was imagining them coming to life.

A shadow detached itself from the edge of the forest. I blinked, and looked more closely. It really was moving, coming slowly towards me – a man. My sword, where was it? I cursed myself that it wasn't to hand.

Before I could react, I was staring into the wild eyes of a tall, dark haired man, whose face was lit by the lamp from my window, and whose skin had the brown, rough texture of the bark of a tree. He had a pointed chin, and some kind of rough tunic, mossy and green. I gasped inwardly as I saw a beetle crawl over his shoulder and disappear down his back.

"Prince Deucalion Stephanos," said the man, in a rustling voice. "We have a message from the People of the Mountains. You do not have much time. You must find the Double Axe, or your kingdom will fall. Find it."

"What do you mean? The Double Axe? Where can I find it?"

"Find the Double Axe, or your Kingdom will fall. The darkness is coming, my prince. Can't you feel it rising?"

He held me with his gaze.

"Tell me more," I said. "Where is it? What is it? How do I…"

But the woodman turned and melted away into the shadows, leaving me gripping the edge of the window.

First Andro, slain in treachery. Then Aster, taken away at night, to the gods knew where. And now the message from the People of the Mountains – find the Double Axe, or your kingdom will fall.

The Double Axe was the symbol of our kingdom. Our priests and priestesses used them at sacrifices, and the woodcutters used simple ones to chop wood – but this must mean the original one, the one that my ancestor, the first King of Crete, wielded when he came to this island. Where was it kept? How could I find it?

I didn't know any of these things.

A thousand questions caught in my throat as I stared out helplessly into the shadows.

7

POWER GAMES

Everywhere I looked, where I stood on the steps in front of the palace, facing out along the royal road, bronze and swords glistened. Horses – not my Swift, thank the gods, I had asked for her to stay behind, as who knew what might happen to her over there in Athens – shifted their hooves, and when I saw the banners unfurl and the double axe of our house spiking into the air I wanted to shout and run and join our army.

My father sat on his horse, facing the horde. He was in his purple tunic, edged with gilt, wearing his bronze armour as the horsehair of his helmet fluttered.

Ari was there too. She picked up a stone and flung it, and the movement reminded me of last year, when an old traveller came to the palace with a wagon, and on it a covered cage. He said he'd come from a land far to the east, where men were dark-skinned and the gods were far more ancient than ours, and cruel. He'd brought a beast back from that place, and he wanted to show it to us.

It was a man-eater, he said, and was striped with flame and soot. Ari and Aster and I were there, Aster frightened, pressing against me.

The old man pulled the cover off and bowed. Aster howled and nestled his head into my side.

A tiger, the old man called it. It had its head on its paws, yellow eyes half-closed. It didn't look like much of a man-eater to me. One of the men standing round said, "But it's just a big cat!" People were about to laugh; a boy even readied a stone to throw. But then it lifted its glorious head and yawned, and I saw its teeth, and it levelled its gaze, and I saw his eyes, and I knew. I felt the tendrils of power in him as he blinked lazily. Everyone stood back from the cage, and the traveller, pleased, bowed. And then the tiger growled, a low rumble that grew until it filled the courtyard. The boy with the stone paused; the crowd gasped. Aster was transfixed, unmoving, unspeaking. Then he wanted to see, and I had to hold him back.

Ari reminded me of that tiger today. She turned to me and smiled. I knew she would be my strength and my ally, whatever happened.

An eagle flew overhead, wheeling far above our assembled army. I saw the seers whisper; the eagle swooped down low out of sight, and reappeared a few seconds later with a hare wriggling in its talons. I took my mother's hand. She seemed not to notice, and I let it go. The seers cried out.

"A good omen! The eagle is Crete, the hare Athens. We shall gain success!"

The men roared and beat their swords against their shields. Dust rose and shimmered in the light.

I wondered how the flight of an eagle could really make things happen.

My father spoke now, and the swords stopped clanging. The sun was high and the palm trees were still. The horses kicked up more dust. My mother put a hand to her face and coughed slightly. She turned to me and smiled, blankly. Pleased at the attention, I smiled back.

"Men of Crete! We go to Athens, not to seek war, but to foster peace. But if the honour of Crete is slighted – then we will fight, and we will fight until we have crushed Athens beneath our feet!"

The men cheered and beat their swords against their shields once more, as the pale sky echoed with the hollow sounds.

My father beckoned me over to him. I walked as proudly and as stiffly as I could, aware that everybody was watching me and wondering if I could be as good a leader as he was. I was wearing a gold coronet on my head, so tight it felt like a vice.

"This is my son, Prince Deucalion Stephanos," he said, lifting my hand and holding it high. My cheeks flushed as the men beat their shields for me too. "I leave him, with Queen Pasiphaë, to rule in my stead. Those of you who remain, pay reverence to them as you would me. Those of you who go with me – think of your own wives, your own children, and bear them in your heart with you, and know that we will come back to our homes in glory!"

He bent down to me and, as everyone cheered, whispered. "And this is for you." He slipped something onto my finger.

It was Andro's ring, and now it fitted me. Swelling pride and honour swept through me. I had to act properly for him, for this man who was not just my father, but a soldier and a king. He released my hand and raised his sword into the sky. The light flashed off it, like from an axe – and the thought pushed my mind to the Double Axe that the mountain man said I should find. Was this some kind of sign?

A piper began his wailing tune and, with my father at the head, the whole cohort, about a thousand men, set off towards the sea, where they would meet the other Cretan cohorts. Only a small garrison remained in the palace. Such was my father's confidence in our power. We watched the soldiers until they were out of sight, and after they were gone the piper's wail still came to us on the breeze.

The others went inside. My mother and I remained.

"He will come back," I said.

She turned to me. Her long hair curled against her cheek. I could smell the scent of oil that she used to wash with, which I'd smelt since I was a tiny child. "If he does not…" Her eyes shifted to the side. She was speaking slower than she usually did, and I wondered at the depth of her grief.

"Then I will be king," I said.

I'd said it. It was the first time I'd let those words out of my mouth, and I tasted them like hot metal.

"My Stephan," said my mother, and she put her hand to my cheek.

"Do you remember," I said, putting my hand to hers, "when we took Aster to see the swans? And how he loved them?"

"I think he wanted to be one," said my mother, and smiled. She coughed a little, and I felt her thin shoulders under my hand. One of her attendants proffered a wrap, but she shrugged it off. "I love to feel the new sun on my shoulders," she said gently.

"Mother…" I said. "Queen Pasiphaë. I saw you with Aster, the other night, going out of the palace…"

She let go of my hand.

"The priestess Myrrah said that nobody should see…"

"Why not?" I said.

My mother sighed. "I cannot say."

"Then where is he?" I said.

She paused, and bent to pick up a wild flower. "He loves these too, doesn't he?"

"Mother…"

"I can't tell you, dear Stephan," she said. "That's something only I, the King and a few others know."

"Then it must be of great importance."

"It is," she said. "Much more so than I can say."

"You won't tell me anything? Even though I'm co-regent now?"

She shook her head. "There is nothing for me to say." For just a moment I saw Ari's set, stubborn expression in her face. "Now we must go in. It's time for our first council."

I sighed. She was right. Duty, always duty. It formed our lives. We ruled well and fairly, and that is why we were kings, and why we were set by the gods over other men. At least, that is what we were taught.

Bansa rollicked up to me as we entered the palace, while my mother's handmaidens remained at a respectful distance, their white garments fluttering like mist.

"What is it?" I whispered. He was jumping from foot to foot.

In as low a voice as he could manage, he said, "I saw Timon and followed him. I found…"

"Tell me later," I said, as my mother turned back to look at me with an enquiring glance.

Bansa ran off, singing to himself, punching at imaginary shadows.

In the small council chamber, not many remained. Those lords who could go to war, and wanted to, had gone. Timon was left, of course; Lord Callias had stayed too. Timon sidled up to me.

"My prince," he said, and bowed, lower than usual.

I nodded curtly. I didn't want to talk to him. He bent towards me, as if imparting some secret wisdom. "I can help you."

I looked at him. He was smiling, a wolfish smile.

"In what way?" I said. He couldn't have heard of the message from the People of the Mountains, could he? Did he know something of the Double Axe?

"There are ways of ruling that I have learnt over the years I've been in your father's service." He smirked. "They laugh about me, the soldiers. They say I am a eunuch." He snorted: "I am no more a eunuch than a lion is."

What could he be hinting at? I said, hiding my feelings as much as I could, "Thank you, Timon." Then I took my seat, and my mother sat beside me, and we began the day's business. It was mostly to do with keeping the supply lines going to the army and the coast.

My mother did not pay much attention to what was going on; I would turn to her for approval, and she would nod her head. She made an excuse to leave before the council's final discussion about arrangements for the Festival of Light. We were feasting that night – the great white hind that we had killed in the hunt was ready to be roasted. It – I couldn't think of it as a she any more – had hung for a while. I felt queasy thinking about it, but I knew that I would have to do my duty.

"All ready for the feast?" said Timon.

"I look forward to honouring Dictynna," I said. "And perhaps she will reconsider her curse."

"Tell me," said Timon, flicking his fingers together in a way that annoyed me, "What do you think power is?"

I thought for a minute. Theo had talked about this with me many times. But I didn't think Timon wanted an answer copied straight out of the mouth of my tutor. I narrowed my eyes until all I could see was a thin strip of the world, shivering and unstable.

"Power," I said, "is the ability to do what is best for others, if they cannot do it themselves."

Timon smiled. "I see," he said. "Perhaps you would like to visit me in my chambers to discuss it further, before the feast? I have some fine wine from the colonies."

Half of me was mortified – a steward, to extend an invitation to a regent – but the other half was intrigued. "You may attend me in my ante-chamber, when the evening star rises," I said, and made what I hoped was a sweeping movement out of the room, leaving him bowing low in my wake. Now that my duties were undertaken, and before the feast began, I wanted to find out more about the Double Axe.

Bansa was waiting for me outside. He'd whittled a small wooden animal – it looked like a hind – and he put it away as I approached. It reminded me, with a pang, of both Aster and of the white deer.

"So tell me exactly what Timon has been up to?" I said.

"I'd been playing with Aisha, the scullery girl, and we were wondering where the sun goes at night," he said, pausing and looking at me with an enquiring glint in his eye, "and I saw Fatty…"

I raised my eyebrows – then realized it was a good way of concealing Timon's name, if nothing else.

"…sneaking out of the kitchen. So I snuck out after him. Where does the sun go?"

"It doesn't matter," I said, smiling.

"Anyway, he went to that place you were talking about, by the Black Lake, and I overheard him saying, 'Have you found anything yet?' and a voice – a woman I think – said she hadn't, but she was still trying, and then they both laughed, and he said, 'And the prince is well?' and she said, 'Prince?' and they both laughed again and then …"

"And then?"

"And then I had to go."

I ruffled him on the head – he hadn't yet been a very good spy, but I could hardly hold it against him – and gave him a small token. He ran off. So Timon had close links with the priestess… And they were plotting something. All these things, weaving together…

Unfortunately I had to go to one of my lessons with Theo. When I got there, Ari was sitting on a stool by him. They were looking at some astrological plans which I'd never seen before. "What is the world made of, Theo?" Ari asked.

"Some say fire," he replied, coughing a little. "Some say air. Some say water, some earth; some say a mixture of all four. Still others say that we are made up of nothing but little tiny bits of matter, which are all the same, and which can't be made or destroyed."

"Are the gods made of the same things?" I asked, joining in.

"The gods exist apart."

"So how do we influence them?"

"Through sacrifice."

"But why would they need sacrifices, if they exist apart from us?"

"You are inquisitive today, Stephan," said Theo. "They are influenced by the vapours and sustained by the fumes."

"So they must be a bit like us."

"Yes, I suppose they must be." He paused, and thrummed his fingers on the table. "I did hear once that there is such a thing as the perfect sacrifice."

"What's that?" asked Ari, shifting forward.

"If it is completed, then a god can be called to earth: and then whoever has succeeded, will have ultimate power over man and earth." He clutched his stick. "But that is just a story, of course. Now, I must put these plans away, as you are distracting us from our real subject matter. The intricacies of our accounting system."

"Theo," I interrupted. "What is the Double Axe?"

He muttered a little, under his breath, leaning his stick against the wall. "The Double Axe? You mean the original?"

"Yes," I answered.

An attendant was sweeping out the room around us. Theo told him to go away, and when the door was closed, he said sharply, "Why are you asking?" His eyes, under their bushy brows, pierced my gaze.

I shifted on my feet. "No reason."

He snorted in disbelief. "These are strange times, Prince. That curse – I have never heard of Dictynna cursing a hunt. I have been looking through all my scrolls, and I cannot find a single precedent – not one. And yet it seems to have found its expression already, in Androgeos's death…"

"Myrrah holds Aster too," I said.

"That there is reason for," said Theo, coughing slightly. "If Asterius is consecrated, then it may avert the curse."

I had a sense of something crouching in the shadows, about to burst out.

"The Double Axe," I said.

"Before this kingdom was founded," said Theo, tapping his fingers against his dry lips, "this was a land of savagery. When your first ancestors settled here from the East, they were beset – not just by natural forces, but by other, darker ones. In desperation, the first King of Crete prayed to his mother…"

"The Mother Goddess," said Ari.

Theo nodded. "Indeed. And she ordered the god of fire to forge him a weapon from bronze, in the fires of the mountains at the end of the world. A double axe. The King faced the evil, and slew it, and cleansed the land."

"Where is it now?"

Theo shrugged his shoulders. "It was buried in the tomb with him."

A great evil. So that was what the Double Axe was for – for defeating something that was ravaging the land. Was Myrrah plotting a great evil, with Timon? To release some darkness from the old times? Had she been communicating with one of the shadow gods?

I shivered. I did not want to go to the tombs, among the bones of my ancestors, and seek out the Double Axe. I didn't even know what great evil it was that I had to stop.

"But you do keep trying to distract me," said Theo, folding away the astrological charts and peering about for his tablets. Now. Accounting."

Ari and I groaned, and the lesson continued until the early evening, when I'd heard as much about accounting as I could ever want.

After the lesson finished, I went back to my room and waited for Timon. I had Bansa prepare some wine, and when Timon arrived, I made sure I was standing up. He couldn't sit unless I did, so I remained where I was. He seemed to me like some spider in the centre of a web, slowly trapping those around him with silky lies.

"To return to our earlier discussion," he said, trying to look as if he didn't mind standing up, while I tried to pass off as haughty. "There is power" – taking a cup of wine from Bansa – "and then there is *power*. There is the sort that you spoke of." He nodded, gracefully, in my direction. "And then there is another sort."

"What sort?" I said quietly. A fly buzzed. Timon lazily swatted it.

"The sort that you glance at in your dreams," said Timon. "The sort that builds, the sort that destroys. It comes from everywhere and nowhere. It changes, shatters, mutates, distorts... controls."

"And are you offering me that sort of power?" I asked.

Timon made the slightest of movements.

"I am merely saying, prince, that it exists." And with that he bowed, and apologized, and said that perhaps we should go, for the white hind was ready, and the feast would be long.

8

THE LABYRINTH

My mother was already in the Great Hall, taking the seat usually reserved for Minos. She saw me come in, but did not acknowledge me. I stopped the hand which I had been about to raise in greeting. Ari, looking restless, was next to her. I caught her eye, but she looked away.

At the table beneath them was Daedalus the master craftsman, looking worn, and tired, and thin. I couldn't imagine my mother being in love with him. He was working at some kind of design on a tablet. I paused to look over his shoulder.

He was drawing a shape that I'd never seen before: a series of lines, all folding into and out of each other. It was strangely beautiful. Daedalus looked up at me, his eyes bright, almost feverish.

"What is it?" I asked.

He blinked, and swallowed. "A… a machine," he said.

I looked at it more closely.

"A machine for what?"

"I am calling it a labyrinth," said Daedalus. "After the labrys, our Double Axe, which it honours."

The Double Axe – his answer had me peering even more closely. "It doesn't look like any machine I've ever seen," I said. What a strange pattern it was - all those lines, twisting and snaking about. It drew me in somehow. I wanted to know more.

Timon was waddling behind me, and he leant over and said: "What about those other designs for the New Temple?"

Daedalus immediately pulled a tablet from a pile near him, and covered up his labyrinth. "This is it!" he said, his manner changing, becoming more relaxed. "I've developed a new method of raising the platform at the edge… and this is how the walls will slide…"

"Thank you Daedalus," I said. "I'll talk to you later about it." Walls sliding, I thought, at the back of my mind. Odd.

With Timon behind me, I marched down the centre of the Hall, reached the High Table and sat down in the plainer chair next to Pasiphaë. I turned towards her.

"Queen Pasiphaë," I said quietly in greeting.

She didn't answer, didn't smile. I looked at Ari, who just shrugged.

It was Timon's duty to start the feast: he clapped his hands together, and silence fell over the assembly. An old man coughed, and sipped from a beaker; a few of the boys my age looked on edge, a couple of them playing dice.

Through the doors came a tumbler, dressed in bright green and red. He turned a somersault, stood on his head and whooped. A few people snorted, but nobody laughed out loud.

The tumbler pressed on doggedly, tweaking the nose of a small boy, who yelped, then leaping over a bench. Somebody shouted.

Then came four men, carrying two poles, and slung between them was the hind. My heart sank. The hind's head, still intact, was placed at the front. I remembered seeing her at bay, killing her, the slap of the spear in her flank, the cries of the men and Myrrah's dreadful voice.

Timon took his place beside me. "And now we shall feast!" he shouted, his oily voice seeping around the hall, and he clapped again. Murmurs started up. One of the boys laughed and, as if on cue, the level of noise rose again.

I watched Timon carving the hind, my face impassive. He offered my mother the first portion; me the next. We poured libations to Dictynna, the goddess of the hunt.

Below, the tumbler turned somersaults. I passed a jug of wine to my mother. She let it sit by her. Why wasn't she talking to me? This wasn't like her at all. Even if she was still grieving for Andro, she was good at keeping up a public face in front of the people.

I pushed the thoughts away from my mind. I wanted to hear more from Timon. I wondered if I could winkle out of him anything that would tell me where Aster was, or whether he'd been involved with Aegeus in Andro's death.

Timon ate noisily, then wiped his mouth with the back of his hand. He took a huge gulp of wine; then, maybe aware that I was staring at him, he blushed slightly. Candles burned in their brackets.

"Tell me, Timon," I said, leaning into him confidentially. "How do you find power?"

I don't know if I imagined it, but for a second I thought he went white.

He patted his wet lips with his fingers. I heard my mother sigh, but at what I didn't know.

"I have long investigated power," he said finally, "trying to understand what it is." The tumbler did a backflip as dogs barked and the boys cheered. I chewed slowly on a piece of venison, feeling its richness, looking closely at Timon. His upper lip was quivering. "But, Prince… I think I am coming to some kind of conclusion." I took a sip of wine.

His eyes shone damply in the dim light. The taste of wine swirled round my tongue, my throat.

"And what is that?" I said.

"Prince! Prince, prince, prince!" He sounded amused, over-familiar. I hated him. "I will reveal all in its due time. But for now – know that I am engaged upon something very profitable. Very profitable indeed." He smiled, and his eyes glittered.

"That is good, Timon," I said. I immediately resolved to find out exactly what it was. "Something profitable for the Kingdom, I hope."

"Oh, very! I have other news for you," said Timon, as the doors swung open again. I looked up to see who it was – and my stomach turned over. Coming up the middle of the Hall was Myrrah. "I have found a new High Priestess." Myrrah came up to the High Table. She bowed low to me and took the High Priestess's seat.

My mother shifted uneasily.

Bansa had heard Timon and Myrrah together – so this was what they were plotting, advancement. The old High Priestess had been ill for some time.

"The tide brings things in," said Myrrah. I bristled, but I could hardly rebuke her. I smiled.

I then turned pointedly from Timon, and talked over Pasiphaë to Ari of other things, joking about the tumbler. Reaching for my cup, and seeing Myrrah deep in conversation with Daedalus, I leant forward discreetly, to catch anything they said.

"Come at midnight," said Myrrah. "Come quietly. We must go over the plans." Plans... perhaps it was something to do with the New Temple – but at midnight?

My mother suddenly shook herself, said, "I will retire," and I, wanting to think more, joined her. As we went past Timon, he bowed low. We exited through the concealed door in the back that led to our private apartments. Ari came scuttling after us, and when we had seen Pasiphaë back to her room, I quickly whispered to her what I had heard.

"I've got to stay with mother," she said. "She asked for me. Go on your own."

I nodded. I would. Who knew what I might find out.

The house of the High Priestess lay behind the temple to the Mother Goddess, which was to the south-east just inside the wall of the main compound. I was beginning to enjoy knowing my way around the palace – this is what it must feel like to be Ari, I thought, when she sneaks out on her adventures.

I reached the inner wall without anything happening, and slipped out. The inner gates weren't locked yet anyway – I whispered to the guard that I'd be back in about half an hour, and he nodded. The red stone pillars of the temple of the Mother Goddess rose in front of me, higher than the residential quarters. The High Priestess's house was at the side, so I slipped around the front of the temple. Then I stopped in my tracks. Standing in front of the door of Myrrah the High Priestess's quarters was an armed guard. No priestess had ever set a guard before. Surely that meant she definitely had something to hide. What were they up to?

The guard stomped up and down, clinking his armour slightly, and coughed, and rubbed his hands together, whistling. He was clearly bored out of his mind. I had half a mind to step out of the shadows and tell him to do his house honour. Instead I looked around for something I could use as a weapon. There were some large chunks of stone lying about, and a couple of good, thick branches. But could I do anything other than irritate him? I wished I'd brought Bansa with me – he'd be able to make a diversion easily. Then I saw a stone nearby. I could throw it into the bushes near him.

I took aim, and hurled it into the side, where it landed, making quite a noise. The guard turned towards the noise, then, whistling the battle march, went to investigate. I ran up to the house and slipped into the door as quickly as I could.

Voices coming from a room up to the right. The rest of the house seemed quiet and empty. I edged up towards the chamber. If I was discovered by someone, I planned to make up some errand from the Queen. But I hoped this wouldn't happen. If they were plotting something untoward, it would only drive them further underground.

I was alone. They might do whatever they wanted with me and nobody would ever find out. Another prince gone. Did they want to kill me and bury me somewhere far away, imprison my mother and sister and leave the kingdom in the hands of Timon? Was that their plan? To overthrow the house of the Double Axe?

The door to the chamber the voices were coming from was slightly ajar, and peeking in I could make out Daedalus. He was standing, and now had an expression of profound concentration and was talking with great urgency. He was bent over something – a scroll, I thought.

"...and this here, you see, is the mechanism by which the pump lifts. And you see these levers and pulleys – they connect to the walls so that they can slide..."

Walls sliding? I thought. Pulleys and levers? What would they be needed for in a temple?

"You are a clever craftsman, Daedalus" – Myrrah's voice, though I couldn't see her from my position. "What they say is true. The space is ready now, for the corridors, for the lines, for the machine. You will start work on this tomorrow. Now go – and remember, do not speak of this, or you know what will happen…"

The lines. Hadn't Myrrah said something about that? The lines filled with blood… And now Daedalus was shivering. So he is doing this under threat, I thought. I stepped back into the shadows as he moved to the door, and watched his retreating back until he went outside. I could see her now. She was standing, a cup held to her lips, with that unearthly fire I'd seen in her eyes before, shining out and somehow making her look metallic, like a gold statue I'd seen once.

"You see," she murmured to herself, "how it all begins. I sought for you in the guts of the beasts. I feel you in me like wind, like fire, like stones. I went to the forest and I cut into an alder with a double axe. It bled like a man, like you told me. I gave you the blood. And then you showed me. The way to all things. The way to change everything, through the lines, through the pathways. The power to form the future, to make the future mine…" She paused, as if waiting for an answer, and then she closed her eyes, and drew her breath in.

Then all the life came out of her, as if it had suddenly been removed and she was nothing but a puppet. She stood, empty.

I don't know how long she stayed like that. I could not move. When she did eventually shake herself and stand up straight again, she let out a huge sigh. Had something entered into her? Was something controlling her? What had she been talking to? Some spirit, some god? The way to all things... I slipped back into the shadows, and held my breath.

She came outside, past me, so close that if I'd wanted to I could have stretched out and touched her robes, and she went to the door and whispered to the guard, who bowed and left; and then she retreated back into her chamber. I waited crouching for what seemed like an age before I dared to creep back out again.

When I got back I found Bansa staring wide-eyed. I put my finger to my lips and got into bed, the image of Myrrah bent over repeated in the shadows on the walls all around me.

9

The Tomb of the King

I saw double axes everywhere I went – in the temple, in the fields; I saw them carved in the walls of grander rooms, or etched into the lines of my palm. The real thing was – perhaps – in the tomb of my ancestor, the first King of Crete. I couldn't delay any longer.

The following night, I put on a cloak, covered my head and took off my ring, which I put in the pouch fastened to my waist. I took a short sword, which I hid under the cloak, and an unlit torch and headed towards the tombs.

In these quarters the corridors were dark. The torches had burnt low, and as nobody came down here much nobody had bothered to relight them. My heart was beating slowly but loudly as I paced along the stone slabs through the shadows. Darkness stretched ahead. I tried not to think about the shadows.

If the Double Axe had been buried with my ancestor, then I would have to go into the sepulchre. Which would mean I would have to see the body of the first King… He would probably be holding it. I would have to take it from the grip of a man who'd been dead for ages. I imagined the skeleton, the bones, the grin of the skull, and shuddered.

As I walked northwards, I couldn't stop worrying that footsteps were sounding behind me. When I stopped at an intersection, I listened carefully. A pounding sound – guards, going the other way. Then a scuttling noise – a rat, maybe. The pounding halted, then moved further away.

A draft blew over my face, chilling me, and causing a tapestry beside me to billow outwards, brushing my hand. I jumped back, then cursed myself. I pulled the cloak tight around me, feeling its warmth, and pressed on.

The corridors were now illuminated only fitfully by torchlight, and the patches of darkness were growing larger in between each small circle of light. I was moving into the deserted areas of the palace. Nobody went to the tombs, apart from at certain times of the year, for rituals. There wouldn't be anyone there now. Though I trod softly, my footsteps echoed.

I was glad I'd brought my own torch, because when I neared the chamber there were no more lining the walls. I fumbled in my cloak for kindling, and struck a flame. How small it looked in the blackness.

There in front of me was the tall door into the chamber that contained the remains of my ancestors. I held my breath for a second, gathered my strength, pushed the door and went in.

My torch cast a smear of light in front of me; just by the door I saw a brazier full of fuel, and thankfully I lit it. Soon it had flared up and the tomb was bathed in a soft orange light. I put my torch in a bracket on the wall, shivering in the cold, and closed the door behind me.

On my left was a platform cut into the rock, bearing a tomb cut in the shape of the Double Axe. To the right was a bench with several objects on it: some three-handled jars, some flasks for holding perfume, a couple of knives, a clay bull's head, a wax royal seal. Was that a whispering noise? Something rustling in the shadows? I shook my head to clear it. There were two double axes, of the kind that the priestesses used, standing on either side of the bench.

It's not those, I thought, gulping. The real thing must be inside the tomb itself, with the bones of my ancestor.

I edged towards the tomb. Thoughts of the shadow gods came into my mind. This was a holy place, I reminded myself. Surely they wouldn't dare trespass here.

All the same I trembled as I approached the tomb. It was made of stone, and it had a heavy lid. Inching closer, I reached out to touch the lid.

The whispering got louder, and I felt the draft again, only this time it was stronger. The door was closed, so how could that be? The flame of my torch on the wall flickered, and I was grateful for the brazier.

Now there was a wind, and it was getting stronger, whipping up dust from the ground. As I tried to get closer to the tomb, the wind pushed against me, and the whispering became sounds of moaning and screaming. The torch shivered and went out.

The force of the gust blew me back against the other wall and I clattered amongst the jars and vessels, knocking some of them to the ground. Winded, panting, I stared at where I'd been moments ago. In front of the tomb, a whirlwind of dust was forming into the shape of a man, hands outstretched.

I couldn't move. It was draped in a long cloak, and it had eyes that glowed with fire and… and it was coming towards me.

Scrambling to my feet, I grabbed at the nearest thing – one of the ceremonial axes – and as the apparition approached me, I swiped wildly – and the axe went straight through it.

Gasping, I reached the door. The thing's cold grasp was on my shoulder, tugging at me and whispering things into my ear, things that made me feel empty and desperate.

This was my home, came the spell. This was where I should stay, among the bones and belongings of my ancestors. I had no need to live. What did it matter that Timon and Myrrah were plotting, that Andro was dead, that Aster was being kept hidden, that my mother was sad, that rumours dogged Knossos?

I turned to face the figure. His eyes were blazing, his robes swirled around him in the dust.

"You are right," I said. "I should stay here…" I prepared myself to accept him, to reach into oblivion.

Then something tugged at the edge of my mind. An image, of Aster, playing in the water, shrieking and giggling.

I can't, I thought. I can't die. I have to face this. I am the son of Crete, I am the heir of Minos.

The figure wavered. "No," I said. "I will not give in. I am here to find the Double Axe of my ancestors, and find it I will."

I sprang towards the tomb, and pushed as hard as I could at the lid. From within came a light that filled the whole chamber with its pulsing. The figure of dust and wind shrieked. I looked inside the tomb – the bones of a king and the tall, golden shape of the royal Double Axe, the symbol of our country.

It came to my hand easily, and as I felt its warmth in my grip I saw my ancestor, the first King, striding forth from the ships that brought him to Crete. Wielding the Double Axe high, I shouted, "Go! Leave this place!" and the evil figure who had tempted me into death's long valley groaned once more, and dwindled away until there was nothing left but a swirl of dust.

I sank, panting, to the ground, and slumped against the cold wall. I had it in my grasp. I had the Double Axe. And if that creature was anything like what I had to face with it, I dreaded what more there was to come.

I was the Defender of Crete.

Except I didn't feel like one at all.

10

An End to Augury

I hid the Double Axe under my cloak and went straight back to my chambers, where I put it in the cedar chest, wrapped up, right at the bottom. Knowing it was there made me feel safer; but it also made me worried. Just as I locked the chest, a knocking at the door made me jump, and I turned round to see that Bansa had come in.

"The beacon fire's lit," he said, more serious than I'd seen him before. I stared at him, knowing what this meant before he told me. "Aegeus didn't accept paying the blood ransom. Our men will now march on Athens."

That night, neither Ari nor my mother appeared at dinner, so I had no chance to tell Ari about Myrrah's meeting with Daedalus, which I was desperate to do; and all the next day I was kept busy with court business by Timon.

"I'd like to see the New Temple," I said, at one point, as we were going through some dispatches about the project that had come from my father, waiting for Daedalus to arrive and tell us more.

"All in good time," said Timon, raising an eyebrow as Daedalus finally appeared in the chamber too. "We are keeping it closely guarded. We do not wish the world to know of our new building methods. There may be spies everywhere!"

"It is a thing of… beauty," said Daedalus. "But also—"

"If we may get to business?" said Timon.

Daedalus put a hand to his forehead, and gulped at a goblet of wine. I could see that he'd been drawing busily on scraps of parchment: all sorts of strange shapes and designs.

"The siege machine has worked very well," said Timon.

Daedalus perked up. "Yes," he said. "I've already thought of a way of improving it…"

"No need, no need," said Timon, and we carried on with the dispatches: after the temple the supply lines, after the supply lines the running of the palace, after that some small matters of justice – a stolen goat, a broken promise – until my head ached and my eyes watered.

It wasn't until two days later that I managed to get Ari to myself. We were standing on the terrace at the eastern side of the palace, looking out over the valley, at the time when the evening star appears. The hills around us were darkening, and there was a slight chill in the air. Ari had just given her last orders to the women of the palace – our mother had taken to her rooms and had hardly come out.

The nearest guard was by the gate at the further end which led back into the main hall. Bansa was at the other end, teasing a cat with a ball of twine. If we kept our voices low, no one would hear us.

"So – more rumours?" I whispered. The constellations started to emerge above us.

"They're saying now that Daedalus and Mother have not just been having an affair. They're saying... Oh Stephan, it's too horrible!" Her eyes glinted in the torchlight.

"Gently," I said. "Tell me!"

"They are saying that Daedalus made something for Pasiphaë, ten years ago, a contraption, a device, so that she could..."

"So that she could what?"

Ari composed herself. "So that she could couple with a bull."

Thunderstruck, I could barely keep my voice down. "Vile!" I hissed. "How dare they say such things? We have to stop them. She can't hear of this."

"It's worse," she said.

"How can it be?"

"They say that she bore the bull a child. And that child is Aster—"

"What?"

"—and that's why he can't talk. And that they've taken Aster away because his... because his horns have started to show." She looked at me, gaping.

"Ridiculous rumours," I said, my mind going back to the gaggle of maids I'd bumped into on the day we heard of Andro's death, how they were wondering how long somebody's horns were – that's what they had been talking about. This must have been going round Knossos for a while, seeded by somebody, for some purpose. But what was the real reason Myrrah had taken him away? Why had my parents let him go?

Far off, a tiny figure was running up the hill towards the palace. The trees were still, the cicadas uncannily silent. The speck became larger.

"He's moving fast," I said. Bansa slipped out of the shadows towards me, leaving the cat to tangle up the twine.

"Like the wind through a horse's hair," said Bansa. He had been learning the lyre lately, and was salting his conversation with phrases from the poets.

The figure hailed us as he approached.

"I come from King Minos," said the man, panting. He held out a token. I took it, and saw that it was a ring with the King's sign on it.

"Your name?" I asked.

"Rusa, of the foot soldiers. I live among the foresters."

I signalled to Bansa to arrange water and food, and beckoned to Rusa, sweating and panting as he was, to follow. This was important – we would have to hear this news in front of everyone. My mother sent word that she was indisposed, but the remaining councillors and Myrrah gathered there in the Great Hall. I felt so small as I sat on my father's throne, receiving the messengers with Ari and Timon at my side.

"Speak, Rusa," I said, trying to sound as much a lord as I could.

Rusa took a deep breath, and looked all around the room, taking in everyone that was there. He looked as nervous as I did. "Athens," he started. "Athens has fallen! King Minos has taken the city, and Aegeus and Theseus are in his power!"

The councillors cheered, and I felt a great wash of relief and a surge of joy. Ari smiled and gripped my shoulder.

"A feast!" shouted Timon. "Spread the news!"

Some of the men took up his cry, echoing, "A feast! A feast!" They called for wine, and servants started running about, pouring goblets and passing around delicacies. Timon drained a beaker, to the applause of those around him. Bansa clapped enthusiastically, and howled like a wolf. From somewhere dancers appeared, and they began trilling in song and swaying for the amusement of the councillors. Rusa was picked up and placed on the shoulders of two guards who paraded him around the room, shaking hands with those who could reach him. They ended at my chair, and Rusa came down, panting slightly, beaming from ear to ear.

Timon rushed off and I thanked Rusa and gave him some gold, then headed off with Ari to see my mother. Such good news – and yet I didn't feel like joining in the celebrations.

My mother was in her bed, gazing blankly ahead. I went to her side and kissed her hand. She moved listlessly. I'd never seen her like that.

"Great news, Mother," I said. "Athens has fallen. Minos will return soon."

She sighed, and motioned me away. What was wrong with her? This couldn't just be grief for Andro. Maybe she was ill?

"You will come to the feast?" I said.

Something of the queen remained in her. She lifted her head. "I will."

I left her, my heart greatly troubled.

That night at the feast, sitting by Ari, who was fizzing with triumph, I watched Timon, Daedalus and Myrrah carefully, but they barely spoke to one another. Daedalus, pale, sometimes glanced at my mother as he drained a beaker of wine. And then another one, straight after. He had his drawings on the table in front of him, and he seemed more intent on them than on anything else.

My heart wasn't in this feast – not when there was treason spreading like a poisonous root, and it was my task to dig it out. I had a strange sensation of things slotting into place, of a great and hideous pattern forming, of something swelling underneath the skin of what I could see. The gods fill everything – that was what Theo had taught me. But it didn't feel that way at the moment. I felt an emptiness, as if they were far away from us, living lives of peace while we toiled beneath them.

I had to leave. I made my excuses to my mother, who smiled a weak smile, and started to go back to my chamber.

As I left, I paused. There was no harm, I thought, in going to Daedalus's room and seeing what I could find there. He'd been looking so nervy tonight. Myrrah had some hold over him, but I couldn't work out what it might be.

Daedalus lived among the lower courtiers, in the north-west of the building near the stores. If I couldn't access the New Temple – was it really so closely guarded to stop spies getting in and stealing his ideas? – I could at least search his quarters.

Once in the wing where Daedalus lived, I pushed open the main door into his apartments. One wall was set with little recesses, out of which poked the ends of scrolls, all tinged with different dyes. I peered at them in the light of the torch – they were carefully labelled by letter, everything neat and orderly.

I pulled out one or two and found lists, sketches of machines, accounts – nothing much to worry about. I was starting to frown at my own foolishness, when the flicker of flame from my torch fell on a scroll that had been put back awry. That's odd, I thought, in a place as neat and tidy as this. More out of impulse than anything else, I poked it back.

A click, and then something swung open in the wall behind me. A panel, gaping wide. My heart began to beat faster. I went towards it and looked inside. There was a whole pile of scrolls in there, some gold, some other bits and pieces. I picked up a scroll and unrolled it.

"...Sacrifice will power it. They will need blood. No more need for augury. They will be the power."

What was this? I had to read on. Trembling, the torch flickering in my shaking hand, I held the flame closer to the text.

"...the control they have over me is too great. She hears the gods, or thinks she does. She has a plan to control the cosmos, to create order and remove chance."

So somebody – they – had control over Daedalus? And she – was she Myrrah? – could hear the gods. But what was this about controlling the cosmos? That meant the world and everything in it: sky, land, sea. And to "remove chance" – we all lived under chance, so it was impossible to do that. Wasn't it?

Something moved behind me. I pushed the scroll back into its place and pushed the panel shut. As I turned slowly around, my flame lit the face of a small boy, gazing up at me.

"What are you doing here?" he said, folding his arms and looking at me squarely.

I edged the panel more firmly closed with my elbow.

"And who are you?" I said, as calmly as if I had every right to be here.

"Icarus, silly," said the boy. He was holding a wooden figure.

"What's that you've got there?"

The boy bent over his doll and held it up to me. It was a man, but no ordinary man – the wings of an eagle sprouted from his back, beautifully crafted.

"Is that one of the wind gods?" I asked.

"No."

"My brother has some of these, but nothing like that," I said. "Now, Icarus, I'm playing a game. It's a hiding game, and I'm going to win. So you can't tell anyone I've been here." I made to pat him on the head, then changed the gesture into a handshake. "Promise?"

He nodded, importantly.

"You go back to sleep now."

He stumbled back to his cot in the corner of the room. Dry-mouthed, I left, shutting the door and leaning against it, panting.

And then I heard the sound of feet, and ran off into the shadows with the strange words of the scroll buzzing in my head like flies around a pail of spilt milk.

"We've got to do something!" said Ari. She was sipping at a little cup in my room.

"What? What can I accuse them of?"

"It sounds like treason to me."

"And what I did sounds like spying."

"You're the regent."

"A just regent? Creeping around my own palace, ferreting out things I can't make sense of?" What should a king be? I wondered. How did Minos do it? He made the laws and controlled the army. Was there any more to it than that? It seemed like there was a lot that I would have to know. Maybe things that I could never know.

I wished heartily for my father to be back, and for my mother to come out of her stupor. For Andro to be alive. For Aster to be safe.

"We have to watch them closely," I said.

"I can do that more easily than you," said Ari briskly. "I'll cloak myself up, and spy on what they're building down at the New Temple. And I'll try to find what hold Myrrah has over Daedalus. Then when Minos comes back, we'll have some evidence."

Fear was slicing through me like a blade. I held her hand. "Be careful, Ari."

She sniffed. "I don't need you to tell me that."

"Daedalus's writings," I said "There's our evidence – why didn't I just take them?"

"I'll deal with it," said Ari. "I'll get the evidence we need."

She slipped away, and I lay on my couch, unable to sleep, sounds and images whirling around my mind, the thought of the Double Axe, lying in my room under my cloaks, its power ready to be tapped.

If only I knew how to use it.

11

The Festival of Light

Ari beckoned to me as I was leaving the Small Chamber the next afternoon. I'd just spent an hour listening to the Steward's men giving me an exact account of the materials used in building the New Temple. I'd tried to listen carefully, but my mind kept wandering.

"Stephan! Let me show you this tapestry I've been working on." She feigned a look of excitement, took my hand and pulled me away from the crowd.

It was indeed a fine piece of work, a scene of maidens weaving cloth in the centre, and the double axe embroidered all around it, and little bulls' heads.

"What are they weaving?" I asked, as a priestess from the old temple walked by.

"They're weaving you," she said, "and me, and Aster, and Androgeos."

"Clever," I said.

She bent towards me. "It's gone," she whispered into my ear.

I smiled at her. "Lovely, sister. I'll use it in my chamber." Then, quieter: "But you found the secret recess?"

"Yes, where you said," she replied. "Only – it was empty."

I cursed silently. Icarus must have told his father that someone had come in, and Daedalus, scared, had hidden the note – or burnt it.

Wincing, I turned away. Either we would have to find some other way to back up our suspicions, without antagonizing Timon and Myrrah, or... I pursed my lips; Minos was coming back soon, on the day of the Festival of Light. Maybe all we had to do was stay out of trouble till he came back, then tell him everything. And I would show him the Double Axe...

"Have you been to the New Temple, Ari?"

She nodded. "Yes. But it's guarded night and day. They said they can't let anyone in, even me. And then one of the priestesses arrived and muttered something about how it has to be kept holy and untouched."

The palace was full of rushings and hurryings.

"We are nearly finished, Prince," Daedalus called as he scurried to his precious temple.

He had bags under his eyes, bigger than ever.

"I hear it's a masterpiece," I said.

Daedalus half-smiled, and seemed about to say something. But then Timon was close by, coughing discreetly for my attention, and Daedalus straightened himself up, bowed and hurried on.

As Timon contrived to have me inspect the stables pointlessly, we went past a group of children making a puppet theatre for the Festival of Light. Icarus was among them, still holding his winged doll, sitting to one side of the group, calm and thoughtful. He had his father's dark hair, but his face bore the imprint of his mother, I guessed. He saw me, but didn't look as if he recognized me.

A boy picked up one of the figures and made it dance, moving it around the small space of the theatre, forcing it to jump; another puppet, shaped like a bull, moved in, and I watched the child make the puppet leap over it.

Was there no relief from those horrible rumours about my mother? I hurried away, feeling as if somebody – or something – was trying to control me, and everything else too.

* * *

"There they are!" Bansa was shouting and jiggling, hopping from foot to foot. Ari, my mother and I were gathered on the palace steps on the morning of the Festival of Light, watching for the first gleam of armour to come up the avenue, the cloud of dust that would come before them. Timon was behind us, and Myrrah was somewhere to our left, surrounded by priestesses; Daedalus was with Lords Nicodemus and Callias, standing to one side in discussion. My heart almost burst with pride as I saw Minos on Farseeker at the head of his army, gleaming and shining like a god.

The soldiers were silent, though: behind Minos was a horse pulling a cart, and on the cart was a body wrapped in a shroud. Andro… and I gripped my mother's hand, and turned to comfort her. She was veiled, and I could not see her expression behind it. She was very still, and she didn't return the pressure of my hand.

Minos reached the end of the avenue, and turned to his army. He raised his sword into the air, and the army roared his name. Then he addressed the crowds waiting on the palace steps.

"My Queen Pasiphaë! My Prince Regent, Deucalion Stephanos! My daughter, the Princess Ariadne! My people! We have returned in triumph. We took Athens in a day, and King Aegeus begged for forgiveness on his knees, and his son Theseus knelt before me."

The crowd roared again, but my father quelled them with a gesture.

"Before we celebrate our victory, we must see our son into the temple of the Mother Goddess. Remember Androgeos."

Four soldiers with a bier came forward and took the body gently from the cart, and placed it on the bier. They walked slowly towards the palace, my father following in the wake of his dead son, and came up towards the steps. The crowd made way for him, and he joined us at the top, bending to kiss my mother and Ari and clasping my hand in silence.

We went with my father to the Temple. Inside the silence, the soldiers laid the body on a slab and quietly departed. The four of us held hands around Androgeos and wept, Ari putting her head on the cold stone.

Later, alone with Minos, he clasped me in his arms – he was my father as well as my king. We were in his small chamber, where he liked to sleep sometimes.

There was a large, covered couch, and not much else but for a bronze sword on the wall and a small statue of a horse on a table by his bed.

"These are the things that make us who we are," he said, as I looked at the horse and the sword. "We break in the horses, and we defend our people. That is why we are the rulers."

Then he held me like he hadn't held me for years, and part of me was happy, but another part of me wanted to shrug him off. I didn't need him to treat me like a little boy. Hadn't I been regent while he'd been away? – and I'd done far more in that role than my mother had. I was nearing fourteen now – almost a man. So I pushed him off, smiling though, so that I could get straight to the point.

"Father," I said. "While you were away—"

"You did well, Stephan," said my father. "Timon has told me everything."

I stopped. Timon had spoken well of me? It didn't seem possible.

"He said you'd learnt quickly, and were very capable. You'll make a fine king one day, he said. And that is a great weight off my mind." Minos clasped me on the shoulder, and moved in for another hug, then changed his mind – and held out his hand for me to hold. I gripped it.

"It's Timon I wanted to talk to you about."

"He said you might," said Minos.

Had Timon got to him already? I had to get straight out with it. "I think he – and Myrrah – are plotting something. Something – bad. They may even have planned the death of Androgeos."

Minos laughed, looked like he might even roar with laughter, but his smile turned sour. "You thought that my trusted chancellor, Timon, planned my eldest son's death?"

"Yes!" I said, wishing I'd thought about it clearly. "I heard him talking about a letter, secretly, in the dark – and Lysias himself said he'd seen a messenger from Crete arrive before Aegeus sent Andro out to conquer the bull…"

"It was a letter I sent," said Minos, frowning. "I sent the letter to Aegeus. It was about a trade alliance that I didn't want anyone else to know about."

"But why would Timon want to know if it had been destroyed?"

"All letters between royal houses are destroyed." He stood up, his chair scraping against the stone, wincing at the pain from a recent wound on his arm. "Now does that satisfy you?"

It didn't. It didn't square with what I'd heard. "I still think there's more to it. This business with Aster, it's…"

My father's eyes flickered with sorrow. "Your brother is safe," he said. "I've entrusted him to the care of the priestess. They are keeping him in sanctuary. Healing cannot be corrupted, Stephan. Now, enough of this – we must prepare for the festival."

He strode out, leaving me, perplexed and annoyed, kicking my heels against the wall.

The mood in the palace was joyful, however, and now that my father was safely back I could hardly help myself from catching it as I ran into Bansa, who was whooping around in one of the courtyards. He jumped at me, and I fought him for a little while, forgetting my troubles.

"I'm going to light the fire tonight!" he said. At the Festival of Light, all the boys and girls of the court lit the great bonfire.

"I'm not allowed to – I have to sit with Minos and Pasiphaë," I said.

"I'll light a bit for you, then," said Bansa. "And what will you wish for?"

"You know if I told you that I'd have to kill you!" I knocked into him, and we chased each other round the courtyard till we collapsed, looking up at the sky.

"Prince Stephanos!" A quavery voice sounded.

"Oh no," I whispered to Bansa.

"Come," said Theo. "You must come and be instructed about the ceremony immediately."

I pulled Bansa up, and went straggling after Theo, looking behind me to make a face at Bansa, who was laughing.

When the evening star had risen, torches were lit all along the passageways of the palace complex. I was wearing a silver moon mask, and I slipped out into the courtyard, watching the other young people cavorting in their own masks – snakes, birds, horses. I dodged a jackal, then ran into a bull, who reared his head up and thundered away. A golden horse was surely Bansa, but then I saw a bronze puppy and thought it was more likely to be him; I chased after him, but it turned out to be somebody else. I'd taken my ring off, and left it in my room, locked in the chest with the Double Axe. Tonight, for a while, I didn't have to be Prince Deucalion Stephanos: now I was just Stephan, a thirteen-year-old boy, a nobody, on the night of the Festival of Light.

At the puppet theatre, a princely puppet was slaying a bull. Poor Andro. If only a story could change things. Forget Andro, I thought. Forget everything, and lose yourself in the music of the pipers and the drummers, in the plucking of the lyre, its strange, liquid, bright music shining like the stars.

The huge fire was to be lit as the moon reached midnight on the longest day of the year. On the raised platform facing it, my parents, Ari and I would stand with some of the more trusted courtiers.

There would be a sacrifice, of course. A bull. I'd seen him in the fields. He wasn't particularly big, but certainly fierce, fiery and red-eyed – I wouldn't want to come up against him. Swift didn't like him either, pawing the ground nervously whenever we went past him.

The lyre music was faster now, wilder, the drummers beating hotly. The pipe was weaving above the lyre, sliding against it, feeding into it. Minos and

Pasiphaë mounted the platform and removed their masks, illuminated by dozens of torches, looking regal and distant.

Myrrah the priestess was in front of the bonfire, unmasked, her face set. The bull was tethered nearby, in a small stockade. I don't know what they had done to him, but he stood sullenly, seeming unconcerned, not even lifting a hoof. Had Myrrah drugged him or something? He snorted, but not very loudly.

I skipped around the unlit fire, weaving in and out of the laughing, masked figures and their waving torches. A drunk man in a stag mask knocked down someone in a bird mask as three little piglets all clustered together, watching, giggling and snorting. The sky was dark and clear and proudly displaying its constellations: the dragon, the queen, the bear. The moon was almost high – gold and silver light, mixed together, shining on everything.

"It's time," came a whisper, taken up by someone else, and someone else, then many revellers all together. "It's time!" At the platform a guard barred my way. I lifted my mask and he nodded me past. I joined Ari on the platform, who was just removing her eagle mask.

"It's time!" Now everybody was chanting it, the words beating to the drum. The pipe had stilled, the lyre too. The bull was untethered, and led to where Myrrah stood, poised and ready. I willed him in his listlessness to bellow, to stamp, to do something…

The young boys and girls who were about to light the fire stood round it in a circle – about twenty of them, all children of the court. They were solemn, suddenly. A priestess, her hair covered, handed Myrrah a bowl of barley, which the High Priestess threw into the huge heap of timber.

Myrrah shrieked. She dipped her hands into some water held out for her, and sprinkled the water over the bull, which sat there stupid and patient. Then, with her dagger, she suddenly cut a tuft of hair off the bull's hide. She hurled the hair onto the unlit fire too.

"It's time, it's time…" came the chant from the crowd.

Two men steadied the bull before the priestess, holding it by the horns. She lifted her dagger and its blade shone.

"A sacrifice to the light!" she yelled – and the children thrust their torches into the heap of wood.

"A sacrifice to the Mother Goddess!"

The whole crowd repeated her cry. The flames in the wood began to catch, criss-crossing, crackling. The boys and girls held hands and danced round the fire as it caught.

"A sacrifice to the lines! To the labyrinth!" she shouted. Caught up in the noise and the heat and the light, I heard the strange new words nevertheless, and listened, uneasily as everybody, fired up by the chanting, shouted it as well.

Only I didn't join in. I didn't like the sound of it. The labyrinth was what Daedalus had called the thing he was working on, the New Temple. Why mention that?

Myrrah stabbed her arm down, slicing the blade into the bull's throat. Finally, something must have reached his dulled brain, because he struggled, and lowed, a mournful call of death.

His life blood was spurting out, spattering Myrrah, who caught some of it in a wooden bowl. It came out in long gouts, juddering, and flowed down the sides of the altar.

The boys and girls ran round the flames as Minos and Pasiphaë held hands and looked out across the square.

An uneasy elation filled me as I stood at the edge of the platform, craning to see the fire reaching its flames into the sky. Myrrah didn't look like a priestess. She looked like something else, something out of the darker stories.

I'd sensed something of that darkness when I'd first gone into the house by the Black Lake, and witnessed the slaughtered beasts in an upstairs room. I shuddered. Something was scratching at the world again, something unpleasant, something deep and old. It was reaching out, creeping into things.

Myrrah sliced with the blade again, and the bull, weakened and confused, fell to its knees.

At the edge of the crowd somebody was bellowing like a bull, and now a man in a bull mask came in front of the fire, capered madly and ran off – it seemed funny at first, but…

"Is that your bull, Queen Pasiphaë?" came a shout. The coarse laughter from some of the onlookers filled the air. I looked at my father. A furious expression was battling to take control of his face. He turned to the guards and motioned with his fingers: seize them, said his gesture, seize these impertinent wretches.

"And when do we get to see him? The Minotaur?"

My mother, pale and graceful, was shaking. Ari and I ran to her, and took hold of her.

"The Minotaur! The Minotaur! We want the Minotaur!" It was hard to tell where the shouts were coming from. "Where is he? Horns too long now! Are you cutting them off, Pasiphaë?"

"Will he eat our children, Pasiphaë?"

"Take me in," my mother pleaded, swaying as we held her. "Now."

"He eats little babies! Have you built the labyrinth to keep him in, Pasiphaë?"

The guards were rushing towards the source of the disturbance, but in the dark, and with the figures all masked, they ran about the place in confusion as people swore that they'd said nothing about the Minotaur at all. Whoever had said those things had run off into the night – or people were lying.

Myrrah, spattered with blood, indifferent to the disturbance, or faking indifference, was staring into the entrails of the bull.

"Power for Crete!" she shouted as we took Pasiphaë through to the palace, a nausea nagging at my throat as the stars wheeled overhead.

"Power for Minos!"

We hustled her up the steps, her handmaidens rushing to our side.

"And power for the labyrinth!"

We took Pasiphaë to her room, and closed the door on that wild and flaming night – on the strange presence that infected the air, on those eerie words ringing in our ears.

12

THE THUNDERBOLT

The sun's chariot had ridden across the sky twice since the Festival of Light, and I was watching Pasiphaë moving the shuttle to and fro on her loom, seated among her rustle of handmaidens in the shady part of the private courtyard near her quarters.

"Mother?" I said. She turned her head slowly and smiled a weak smile.

The words to comfort her wouldn't come. We hadn't been able to keep the horrible rumours from her. After losing Andro, it was too much for her. Her eyes were as mechanical as the spindle she held. She dropped it as I reached for her, and Isis, the girl from Egypt, bent down to pick it up, pursing her lips at me in warning.

Ari touched my hand. "Come on. Father wants us." I took one last look at my mother, and I thought of the three sisters who spin our life threads and choose when to cut them off – Mother used to tell me about them when I was little.

Timon was whispering something into my father's ear when we came in to the small chamber. He withdrew hurriedly. The Lords Nicodemus and Callias were standing on either side of Minos. I felt a presence to my right – Myrrah, crouching on the floor in the shadows – and fear went curling up my back.

"We are discussing the conquest of Athens," said Minos, gruffly. His eyes were elsewhere, distant, his voice lower than usual. "We have come to good terms with Aegeus."

"It is not enough," said Lord Nicodemus. "We should have pulled down every stone of that cursed city. We should have killed every man, woman and whelp."

"It is a just settlement," said Callias, cutting over him with his deep, gentle voice. My father was gripping the arm of his chair, his knuckles whitening. A silence grew in the room, as thick as the tapestry in the Great Hall.

A weird gurgling from Myrrah as she sprang to her feet cut through it all. I caught Ari's hand.

"Blood! The gods demand blood!"

Everybody froze. My father raised his hand, about to say something.

"She is entranced by the gods," hissed Timon. "You must not stop her, it would bode ill."

"I see them," she said. "Their shapes are in me. I am the shadows. They speak through me!"

She was standing upright now, her eyes flashing fire. Her voice grew lower. "The lines need blood. The lines make the world. Oh scarlet tide! Oh arrow of starlight! They pierce me! The lines demand blood, from the King of Athens. A royal child has been killed. The land will die if the lines do not have blood!"

She gasped, and clutched her throat. "A prince inside the lines. The lines filled with blood. Take blood, Minos, from Athens! Take their children! A prince will heal." Her voice was clearer now, but still it sounded as if it came from somewhere far distant. "I see waste without blood! War without blood! I see the world falling apart! I see the crushing of things! I see wounds filled with light! I see a split!" She was talking in a toneless mass of sounds, all pounding in my ears.

Minos barked, "What do the gods want?"

"Seven beardless youths of Athens. Seven pure maidens of Athens. Their blood will heal the prince. Their blood will cure the world!"

She staggered and I ran to catch her before she hit the stone floor. She felt limp in my arms, as if she were asleep.

"What does it mean?" Minos was commanding, turning to Timon.

"My king," said Timon. "The gods say that, in order to atone for the death of your royal son, Athens must pay tribute to you."

"Yes, yes," said Minos. "I understood. But – what form of tribute?"

Timon faltered, but I understood: a procession of boys and girls, barely older than me. Maybe everything had always been leading to this moment. All those twisting pathways were folding into straight lines. Into the labyrinth.

"Seven young men, my king. And seven maidens. To be… sacrificed. To atone and, by atoning, to heal the prince."

"To heal Asterius?"

"The gods will heal Asterius if the sacrifice is made. It is restitution," said Timon.

I was finding it hard to breathe.

"They deserve it," said Nicodemus, loud and boisterous.

"It is just," said Timon.

I held Ari's hand tight. She was about to speak, when Minos said, "You ask for human sacrifice? You ask King

Minos of Crete to return to ways that have not been known for generations? It's impossible!"

Myrrah stirred, and I released her. She stood before the King, and when she spoke, it was in her normal voice.

"It is not I that ask, my king, but the gods."

The chamber seemed filled with noise, somewhere just at the edges of my hearing, a whispering, a murmuring.

"I will not allow it," said my father fiercely. But there was something else in his voice, something that I hadn't heard before. It sounded like defeat. "That is a barbaric custom – a custom that we find appalling!"

"You understand, my king, what will happen if the gods are not satisfied?" said Myrrah.

"I do not, Priestess," said Minos, softly.

"Then I will tell you." She closed her eyes, and breathed, slowly and heavily.

"She is communing with the gods," whispered Timon to me. I went to my father, and put my hand on his shoulder, but he shrugged it off. It looked to me like Myrrah was entering a trance – before long she looked like nothing but a horribly lifeless puppet.

"…need sacrifices… to make the power… if no sacrifices… then the destruction of the house of the Double Axe. Plague and pestilence and death."

We all looked at her, held in a net of fear.

A rumbling – and the frame of the palace seemed to be shaking. At first I thought I was imagining it, but everyone in the small chamber was glancing up to the walls.

"The death of the princes, the death of Minos, the death of Crete!" Her voice got louder and louder, screeching and shrieking, until it sounded as though there was more than one voice.

There was a noise, like something crashing, and I swear that the whole palace shook. I held on to Minos's chair for support. He groaned. I'd never heard that sound before.

"Death to the house of Minos!" came Myrrah's voice over the crash.

Everything shuddered, then was still, as though an earthquake had passed.

Then somebody ran in and said, "Outside, outside!"

And Minos was shouting, "Out! Out, all of you, out! Take the priestess with you." Ari and I went to him, but he waved us away, so I pulled Ari away with me.

We all ran out through the passageways, out to the southern steps of the palace, where a small crowd was gathering.

"Look! Look!" It was Bansa, pointing ahead.

There on the ground was a charred, black pit, smouldering.

"They say it was a thunderbolt…" said Bansa. "They say the gods are angry!"

"A sign!" shouted Timon. "A sign that the gods must be satisfied!"

The crowd took up the call, all shouting and chattering amongst themselves.

"The gods! The gods must be satisfied!"

Myrrah was standing on the steps of the palace, surveying the crowd.

"The High Priestess! The High Priestess!" they called. "The gods are angry!" she shouted. "The gods will have their due! And we will get that due from Athens!"

"From Athens!" shouted the crowd, running around, becoming frenzied

"Your crops will be saved! Your livestock will be saved! Your children will be saved!" shouted Myrrah. "When the tribute comes from Athens!"

"From Athens!" yelled the crowd again, as Ari and I turned to each other, dismayed.

There was only one person I could think of to go to for help; but whether I could find him was another matter.

"I can feel things… slipping," Ari said to herself softly.

I shook her by the shoulder. "Ari, come with me."

We left the swelling crowd, gaping and gasping round the palace, and ran into the forest. As we came into the shade of the trees, we could hear the cries of the people behind us. As we went further in, I could only hear Ari's breathing, and the rustling of the wind in the branches.

I ran fast, and Ari kept pace with me. I didn't know where I was going, but I had a feeling that, if I called, he would come.

We came into a clearing, and I stood in the centre, turning around slowly, looking up into the trees. "Help me! People of the Trees, the heir of Crete calls you!"

All around us, branches were waving in the breeze. Forest creatures would be slinking away at my noise, scuttling into their burrows. There was a thick, musty smell, earthy and rich.

"People of the Trees! The heir of Crete calls you!" The words rang around the glade. He won't come, I thought. I looked at Ari – her mouth was wide open in wonder. I followed her gaze.

There, by the edge of the clearing, was the woodman. He came further in. He seemed from a distance to be nothing but twigs and leaves, but as he came closer I could see again that he seemed like a person, but with bark-like skin. He moved strangely, feeling the ground first with his foot, as if he was considering putting down roots.

He came within arm's length of us. We bowed to him, and he inclined his head. There was something in his eyes, black as they were, like berries, that I'd never seen in anyone's gaze before. Something wild and strange. I could almost hear him creak as he moved. "The darknesses…" he whispered, his voice like scratching twigs.

"What is it?" I asked quietly.

"In her, they are not true."

"Tell us," I asked, gently, almost reaching forward in my haste.

I must have crossed some kind of invisible barrier, because he suddenly snapped his teeth together and his eyes flickered – the People of the Mountains were not to be trifled with.

"In her the darknesses are false," he whispered again. "In the priestess there is no priestess."

Myrrah, wanting us to take tribute from Athens. Human sacrifice. The thunderbolt. Fire from the sky... but was it the sky, or had it come from beneath the earth? My head reeled.

The man hissed, and bowed, and retreated, and we were left alone together in the clearing, looking at each other in dread.

"We have to stop this," I said. "We can't let it happen. Any of it."

"We can't," she said, and our voices sank into the air.

13

The Gifts

"I've got something to tell you." Bansa was hugging himself tightly, and nodding his head up and down.

"What is it?" I knew I was irritable. My head ached after an hour with my father, Timon, Daedalus and Myrrah working on the details for the ceremony for Andro's burial. Overwhelmed with grief and frustration, I'd escaped to my room to recover.

"You know how you told me to come and tell you if I saw anything suspicious?"

I nodded, though my mind was too full of strange things to pay attention, and his words drifted through me.

"...can lift a horse? And I said I bet he couldn't and he said he could so I went with him down to the..."

Myrrah had sat through the funeral arrangements with her face set. I was afraid of her, more than I could say. Minos was silent too. Timon had been doing all the talking.

"…and then I saw Asterius. And he couldn't lift a horse anyway."

"What?"

"Well he's only ten."

I leapt on Bansa. "Where? Where did you see him, you idiot?"

"I told you, in the New Temple."

"How did you get in?"

He shrugged. "No one notices us much. We snuck past the guard pretty easily."

"Bansa!" I almost hugged him. "Are you sure?"

"Yes, I saw him as clearly as I can see your stupid nose."

I let that pass but still shook him a little, partly from joy, and partly from annoyance.

"Ow!" he squawked. "Do something nice for you and all you can do is shake me…"

I released him. He continued to chatter and shake. There was something about Bansa that meant you could never be cross with him for long. "Can you take me to him now?"

"Hmmm… I don't think so," he said, grumpily, hugging himself. "They didn't look like they wanted to be seen."

"Who?"

"Myrrah. And some other people."

"What kind of other people?"

Bansa looked at me reproachfully. "I don't know! Priestesses and things. And a guard."

That was enough. I had to confront her, now.

A few moments later I burst into the room where Myrrah sat, hunched over a burning coil of incense. She looked small, shrivelled, as if something had been removed from her. Around her was a mess of parchments, and little models of things. She was pouring water into a funnel; as I stood before her I watched the water flow through a series of runnels in a piece of wood, to collect in a pool. Carefully, Myrrah lifted the piece of wood, and poured the water into a jug.

"Asterius, the prince. My brother. What are you doing to him?"

She stayed so still, her eyes sunken. The smell of the incense was dizzying. I started to think she wasn't properly awake. Or alive. And then, with awful slowness, she swivelled to face me.

"It is not for you to know, Prince," she muttered. "The King knows, the Queen knows, but some things are not for little boys."

The shadows cast over her face made her expression hard to read. "It is!" I bridled, fighting my fear. "It is for me to know! I am the heir to Minos and I must know!"

She came into a patch of light, her eyes glowing deeply.

"Very well," she said, her voice still thin and toneless. "But knowledge can be more harmful than innocence." She clasped her hands together – skeletal, white hands.

"Tell me."

She stood up, unfolding and cracking her bones as her robe fell about her in folds.

"He will live inside the lines."

"What do you mean?"

"The lines inside the New Temple. The labyrinth. Power flows through the lines. Power of more than one sort. When the sacrifices are complete, then Asterius will be healed and balance will be restored."

The tribute from Athens – girls and boys to be human sacrifices. "So many people dead?"

"It is what the gods want," she said. "You've seen their power. The thunderbolt. Imagine what they can do if they don't get what they want. Now go."

"Can I visit him?"

She shook her head. "He must be kept pure."

I left with my thoughts in turmoil. My brother – healed! Made whole! But at such a price? Seven young men, and seven maidens… Minos and Pasiphaë must have approved it by now. Did it make a horrible kind of sense to them? One prince lost, one prince remade… In my heart I felt sick at the thought of those sacrifices. What if it had been us, conquered by Athens? What if it was me? No – I had to stop this. It was tearing me in two. And Myrrah – she was hiding something, I knew it.

* * *

The day of Andro's burial arrived. It was nearing the end of summer, and the people of the palace were busy preparing the storerooms for the harvest: something in which I was supposed to take an interest – but in fact I could hardly conceal my boredom.

My father, who would usually be overseeing preparations, had become withdrawn, leaving his councillors to deal with Athens. He was now almost as absent as my mother, so it was unfortunately down to me to make sure that everything was being done properly. I decided on this occasion to let Timon take charge, even though I was sure that he was creaming off some of the harvest for his own use.

Andro was wrapped in a shroud and laid on a bier in readiness for his journey to the tombs – the tombs where the strange apparition had tempted me with death. Would it be waiting for Andro? Maybe he was the one who needed the power of the Double Axe.

The priest who'd performed the sacrifice when Aster was born was leading the procession. I was glad it was him. The sky was white. The salt smell from the sea was strong. The men bore the bier with Andro's remains up the steps into the palace, and we followed.

My brother Andro, so strong and brave, now a thing wrapped in white about to be put into the tombs. I looked at Ari – she wasn't crying; none of us were. Minos was impassive; Pasiphaë, veiled heavily, with her usual guard of women around her, as still as a statue.

The priest set up the chant of mourning, and I joined in quietly. Unable to bring myself to look at Andro's remains as they were lowered into the tomb, I turned my gaze to the wall. The priests' chants rose to a pitch, echoing and filling the chamber, and then there was nothing. Androgeos, Prince of Crete, dead, placed in the cold stone.

Outside it was time for our mourning rituals to begin. But as we gathered we saw there was something snaking down the hill – a mass of shadows, it looked like, moving quite quickly. I blinked, wondering if it was just my sight, troubled by grief.

But no… There was definitely something there. It looked like an immense creature – but how could it be? Nothing could be that large, that long. It was still far away. I tugged at Ari's sleeve, and pointed with my chin. The priest's voice faltered above the growing noise of murmurs.

The mass in the distance was becoming more distinct – not a single thing, but a procession of… of what? Not people. As they came closer, they gave off a shimmering radiance whiter than the sky. Things around them seemed to blur a little; you couldn't look at them straight. My heart was hammering. "What is it?" I said to Ari.

Her eyes fixed on the moving procession. "I don't know," she said. "But it's beautiful…"

Some of our people had broken ranks, and were running to the priest, shouting questions at him. The beings coming towards us were closer now, their hair flowing in a breeze that did not touch us, some of them looking like they were made from leaves, stones, even water.

Ari whispered into my ear. "It's the People of the Mountains!" But I had already guessed.

"I remember," I said. "They come at the funeral of the heir to Crete."

"There's another part to the story," said Ari. "I remember my nurse telling me about it."

The hair on my head tingled with power. A cleaner, kinder power than the one I'd felt at the Festival of Light, but also wilder. My heart was thrumming and my mouth was dry. I couldn't see how many there were – they seemed to slide in and out of the landscape they passed through. Three at the front were the most distinct, their young faces containing eyes old and mournful. There was something metallic in the air. Was this what it felt like to be too close to a god?

A strange hush enveloped us like mist. Every mortal face was gazing at the procession of the mountain peoples.

Minos and the priest had come to the front. Minos gathered his purple robe around him, and then, slowly, he knelt, until his head was touching the ground. The priest followed his example. We all, as one, obeying a signal we felt but did not hear, pressed our foreheads to the ground.

"Rise, Minos," said a voice, like the scratching of branches in the wind. I could see nothing but a small space of earth. My breath was hot.

"Rise, people of Crete."

Those faces, so familiar, but still so odd.

"We are honoured," said Minos, "that the People of the Mountains come to us."

"To the funeral of Androgeos we come," said the woman with skin like bark, her words rustling softly.

"The body of Crete's heir is in the tomb," said the man whose skin was translucent like water. I could see thin veins pulsing.

"The children of Crete are in the balance," said the other, cool and flinty.

"Let the princes and the princess come," said the woman with skin like bark. A knot tied itself in my gut. Me? Ari and I crept forward, without speaking. There was some kind of force around these people – we could not stand too near them. I was sweating, but I was freezing cold at the same time.

"Where is the other?" said the woman, her voice scratching and whispering.

"Prince Asterius is being healed," said Minos.

A shadow passed over the faces of the mountain people. They seemed to shift into somewhere else, and then back, to flicker for a breath. I wondered how it felt to be like them, immortal.

They stretched out their hands. The bark-skinned woman called to Ari and placed a short, slim object into her hands.

"Prince Asterius." The bark-skinned woman now called. "Prince Asterius." The name rang out over the courtyard. Nobody dared to say anything as the woman turned to me. Her eyes were so full of strength that I felt myself on the point of collapse. "Give this to Prince Asterius," she said, and handed me a long, broad, hard thing covered in bark and leaves.

"Prince Deucalion Stephanos, heir to Crete."

I went forward to a third member of the mountain people, ready to receive my own gift, trembling.

"You have had your message, you have found your task," she said quietly.

She bent forward and touched my head, and I felt her power rush through me. I waited for my gift – but none came.

The three held hands, and danced round in a circle three times, singing in voices that sounded like the world itself come alive, songs that hinted at the birth of things and the death of everything. It felt like whole forests and oceans and mountains grew and fell.

When they finished we all stood, unmoving, having shared in something wonderful that was now ended. A woman stretched out her hand towards them, as if to say: "Take me! Take me!" And then she retracted it.

The three rejoined their shadowy procession, and flowed off, back to the mountains, to the woods, to the streams. And we watched them go.

Ari and I went to my father, who stood still under a pavilion, looking at the sky. Perhaps he was recalling when he'd received the statue of Talos: he had inherited the kingdom when he was nine years old.

His face was blank, but beneath that I could sense that he was troubled. Ari and I sat on either side of him, and placed the two objects carefully on the table that was next to him.

Each was wrapped in bark.

Ari unwrapped hers first: a long knife, with a snake's head carved into the hilt.

Minos gazed at the fine workmanship, and said, "A fine gift. It is for your protection, and your intelligence."

I started to open Aster's.

"No!" said Minos. He looked like he was struggling to speak. "Asterius must open it himself. You do not trifle with the gifts of the People of the Mountains. Keep it for him," said my father. "Keep the gift for Asterius." He pulled his robe around him and looked down at the ground.

"And what about yours, Stephan? Why was there nothing for you?"

I didn't know what to say, and could only watch as he swept off, leaving Ari and me sitting under the white sky.

14

THE COMING OF THESEUS

I put Aster's gift in with the Double Axe, in my locked cedar chest. What Ari did with her dagger she didn't tell me, but it made her eyes fiery. One day – soon, I hoped – I would understand all these things, and know what was to be done.

A few days after the Peoples of the Mountain came, my mother summoned me to her chamber. She seemed weak, but a little more lively. "My darling Stephan!" she whispered, propped up on several pillows. A candle burned on a polished wooden table by her bed. Tapestries hung on the walls, showing scenes of hunting and play.

She stroked my face. "You must learn not to let tittle-tattle get to you… You know these things are not true."

"I know, Mother," I said.

* * *

"That's him!"

"He's so good-looking!"

"So handsome!"

"They say his father is a god – the sea god!"

"Imagine!"

Bansa and I were walking past a group of maids, on our way to a lesson with Theo. They were grouped around a large open window, giggling as a procession climbed the long winding path below to the main palace doors. Bansa leapt up onto the window sill for a better view.

"Hmph," he said. "Well I think he looks like a squashed vegetable."

One of the maids – a pretty, fair-haired girl, with light-blue eyes and a wry smile – giggled. I think Bansa liked her.

There was a train of horses approaching, and four wagons behind them which were laden down with baggage. A strange thought struck me: why bring luggage with you on the way to your own death?

On the leading horse was the man the girls were laughing about: Theseus, the prince of Athens, Andro's friend. King Aegeus had sent him. A prince for a prince.

Theseus was riding a grey horse even more beautiful than Swift. He rode alone, in front of the others. He didn't have a face like a squashed vegetable, not at all. He was tall, with much paler skin than we were used to in Crete, and hair as black as storm clouds. He looked in our direction and for some reason I flinched.

A defeated enemy, coming in tribute to us – I should have been filled with triumphal glory and the love of Crete. Why wasn't I?

Behind Theseus rode two sets of three young men, all with a noble, courtly bearing, and all wearing armour, like Theseus, though none were armed. They looked like any of the young men who haunted the court, lounging about the dancing floors, showing off on the wrestling ground.

After them, also in two sets of three, came the girls, dressed as Dictynna the hunt goddess might dress, in purple boots and doe skins. Theirs was a beauty I had not seen before, and it struck me right in the heart. Keeping the rear was a seventh, proud-looking girl with strange red hair and skin so pale it was like a summer cloud. Seeing Bansa gasp, one of the maids dug him in the ribs

"Don't think much of her." She and her friends went laughing on their way.

My father Minos stood at the top of the steps to receive the tribute, his face grave and sad. He stayed so still these days, like a statue of a king rather than a king. A circlet of gold gleamed on his head. On the staff in his left hand glowered the sacred bull's head.

At the bottom of the steps Theseus raised his hand, as if in supplication, and then dismounted without completing the gesture.

"Greetings, King Minos." His voice was tinged with something foreign, but it rang out proudly. "They say my father is the sea god, and that yours is the god of the sky. They are brothers. We, then, are cousins by the blood of the gods."

Close up, Theseus had a finely shaped face which looked as if it had never seen the sun. And yet he was well muscled. Ari was looking at him intently.

"We have come to you, willingly, as tribute. The gods asked for seven young men and seven maidens. And here we are." He bowed, a little ironically. "What the gods ask for is often obscure. But we are bound to obey them."

Minos nodded. "Cousin, royal prince, Athenians. While you are with us, we will see to everything that you need." He signalled to Timon, who sprang forward with other stewards and grooms to lead the Athenians away.

I couldn't bear the formality and pretence of it all. I wanted Theseus to storm and rage and curse, and the girls to rend their hair and beat their breasts. But instead, icy and upright, they walked calmly up the stone steps, and closer to their certain deaths.

But everything that was happening seemed strange and far off, as if I was watching it in a dream. Watching Theseus walk through the huge open doors of the House of the Double Axe, all I could think of was Myrrah's blade falling onto the neck of the bull; and those carcasses in the house by the Black Lake; the staring eyes of the foal.

The Great Hall was full, and the people were silent. There, at the foot of the throne of Minos, stood the fourteen Athenians. Theseus and the flame-haired girl were aloof and apart. The others clustered together, so beautiful and strong and healthy. They looked like they could be my friends. One of the men winked at me as I came up close and put out his hand. "Pallas," he said.

Pallas was tall, and had blond hair – like the sun god, I thought, stupidly. His smile dazzled as he pointed to the flame-haired girl.

"Daphne."

And she was beautiful. She took my hand. I gulped. Why couldn't I say anything? This wasn't like being with one of the girls of the court, or the serving girls.

Daphne smiled at me and released my hand. I could sense hundreds of eyes on me and hoped that they couldn't tell how hot and embarrassed I was. I blushed. Now they could, I thought. Bansa, in the crowd, waved at me.

"So you're the heir to Crete?" Daphne said.

A slight note of mockery in her voice.

I nodded, ignoring Bansa who was pulling faces. "Er… yes… Welcome to Crete!" I said.

"I hear you're a *fine* shot" – again, that note of sarcasm that made my cheeks flush.

Luckily Ari came to rescue me, introducing me to all the others, their names rolling past me like waves. First a striking white-faced blonde girl called Philoclea who raised her eyebrow at me. And this was Corin, whose brawny arms looked like they could break a tree trunk in two. Here was Damon, lean and bright as a sparrowhawk. Resting on a pillar with her arms folded was dark-haired, flint-eyed Helena; and more, one after the other, all handsome or beautiful, and quick, and strong.

What could I say to them? I shook each of their hands, and was left with Theseus, standing at the foot of the throne of Minos.

"The heir to Athens and the heir to Crete," said Minos.

Theseus was much taller than me, and better-looking, and more muscled. I bowed my head to him, and he did the same.

He clasped my hand. "Cretans! We come in tribute. I am here to atone for the death of your heir, Androgeos. But in your new heir, I see greatness to come." The crowd roared and applauded, Bansa cheering louder than anyone as Ari looked on unsmiling.

Greatness to come, I thought. Not now, but still to come. So confident he seemed, and serene. Hopefully I would act the same in his place – it would not do to show fear, or anger.

He let go of my hand, and then leant in to whisper to me. "Assuming, Your Royal Highness, that you last long enough." His eyes flashed, and I felt a red mist of anger descending. He was goading me: but I would not let him win. I gulped away the rage.

The crowd pulled him away – I caught one last sight of Daphne, who inclined her head to me as they headed for their quarters, where they would rest before the feast.

I had a sick feeling in my stomach. How could we sit with these people, eat with them, knowing that two by two they would be sent into the temple to be killed? Daphne, Philoclea, Pallas – and even Theseus himself.

Couldn't I stop this? I needed to know more about the history and practice of sacrifice. I needed to go to the records room.

It was dark in the library, and all the scholars who would normally be working there had gone to the tribute. I didn't want anyone to know I was there, so I lit only a little taper and held it close to my chest. I felt crammed, hemmed in; the small flame threw large shadows. It always felt like someone was watching you, in the House of the Double Axe, and I could sense some kind of mind focused on me. I shook off the idea – a ridiculous one – and went further in.

I hadn't spent much time in the records room before, but I knew how it was organized: like in Daedalus's room, the ends of the scrolls were tinted with dyes.

But I didn't know which ones were which. Stupid, I cursed. I pulled out a scroll at random, its end the hue of the summer sky.

A list of clothing ... How could I ever find what I was looking for? My small light flickered. Something scuttled in the corner. I bit my lip. Think, Stephan, think. There was a kind of dark colour, like blood when it first came out in drops, which the priests wore at special feasts. I brought the light along the lines of scrolls. The grass. The summer clouds. Winter sky. There – a blood red. I pulled out a scroll – yes! It was a sheet of invocations to the gods. Hymns to the Mother in all her aspects, asking, imploring for health, fertility, fine crops – all the things that made our island grow and flourish.

Sacrifice was a form of asking. We begged the gods for things, and sometimes they granted them and sometimes they didn't. My father and mother had asked the gods for a cure for Aster. But it hadn't happened. And Myrrah had promised Aster would be cured by the sacrifice of the Athenians, but how could she be sure? We were at the mercy of the gods – we couldn't control them. With sacrifice we called on the gods to help us. But did they want to help us?

I put the scroll back, and looked through the others: more hymns, more invocations. Just as I was beginning to think I would never improve my understanding of so mysterious a matter, I picked up a third scroll from the end, and unrolled it.

I looked closely at its strange lettering, frowning. It took me a while to realize – it was written backwards. At that moment I heard the door open and the noise of people coming in; lights too. I blew mine out and hurriedly stuffed the scroll into my tunic as I fled.

Back in my room I searched for the polished bronze that I sometimes used as a mirror, but couldn't find it. Then I remembered the Double Axe. I flung my clothes out of the trunk and there it was, just as I'd left it, wrapped up in linen. I carefully unwrapped it and saw my face, distorted, looking back at me from its gleaming blade.

I unrolled the scroll and held up the bottom of it so that it was reflected in the blade. "To conjure the shadow gods, there are darker rites, for which a greater sacrifice is needed. This is not right, and against all principles of priesthood. It means human sacrifice. The darkest gods need royal blood."

My heart stilled. Shadow gods – controlling the worlds. Royal blood. That's what Myrrah wanted to do: sacrifice these Athenians and call up a dark shadow god she could control. And now I understood what she meant when she'd said the sacrifice would be complete. Complete meant Aster. A prince of royal blood to complete the sacrifice.

She'd kept Aster all this time in order to kill him.

Myrrah and Theo and Timon were suddenly behind me. I stood up, my new knowledge burning inside me, and quickly concealed the Double Axe and the scroll in the chest, packing my clothes gently above them as if I had just been disturbed looking for something, locked the chest, then turned to them and said quietly, "You attend me?" I could hardly contain myself.

"Prince," said Timon. "The gods have spoken in Myrrah. You must come with us."

What was this? Theo was looking at the ground.

"Where?" I said. "The feast?"

"Prince, you must follow us." Timon began to leave, waddling.

"This is outrageous. You can't command me like that," I said.

Then Myrrah spoke, her voice deep and old. "The prince and the princess must be kept in holy sanctity during the sacrifices. Otherwise they will be polluted."

"What?" I exclaimed. "Where is Minos? And Pasiphaë? Do they know about this?"

"They know, Prince," said Myrrah. "Now, will you come with us or will we have to call the guards?"

I wanted to shout – but she was a priestess, and inviolable. I couldn't touch her. The penalties for harming a priestess were harsh. Theo caught my gaze, resignation in his eyes.

"I heard it, Prince," said Theo. "The gods are calling for you and your sister to be placed into holy sanctuary while the sacrifices happen. I'm sorry, Prince Deucalion Stephanos. But the gods command it."

The gods, I thought. "In her they are not true" – that's what the woodman had said. She was twisting things, or else something false was coming from her.

Six days remained. Six revolutions of the sun, before that flame-haired girl Daphne and that handsome prince Theseus were sent to their slaughter, and the gods knew what would come billowing out of the earth to destroy us all, at Myrrah's command. Couldn't I run away from my captors, escape, find Minos, who would stop this?

But would he? He was in thrall to Myrrah, to the idea of Aster being healed, to the idea of power over Athens. And then – to be a fugitive in my own country? It would not work. I would have to go with them, for now.

"Very well," I said, my heart boiling with emotions. "Let us go."

15

TRAPPED

The door slammed and the key turned. Ari was already there, chafing like a caged beast. We'd been taken to a small set of rooms in the northern part of the palace, quite cut off from everywhere else.

"They just turned up as I was dressing," she said. "They were very polite. I tried to go and see Father, but they said…"

"I know," I replied. "They've got a hold over him, and over Pasiphaë."

I told her about what I'd read in the library.

"So this, this New Temple, these human sacrifices, they're all some kind of ritual to call up a shadow god?"

"I think so," I said.

She looked at me, terror in her eyes. "And what about Aster?"

I had to tell her. And I did.

"She's going to kill him."

Ari moaned and covered her face with her hands. I went to hug her, but she pushed me away, breathing deeply.

A little while later she looked up at me, her face pale and blotchy.

"We've got to get out of here," said Ari grimly. "We can't let this happen. It's a huge conspiracy. They – Timon, Myrrah – have been lying to us, to Minos, to Pasiphaë. They can't kill Aster. He's ill! He's a little boy! He doesn't know what's happening to him!"

"So what can we do?" I asked. "Let's look around."

There were four chambers in all – one with a big, soft bed that I assumed was for Ari, and a room with a smaller, harder one for me. There was the room we'd been put into, where we could sit, which had a table; and another one, with space for washing and a tiny latrine in a cupboard. I looked at the hole, but it was too narrow to squeeze through.

There were only two windows, and they were narrow and high up. No one could climb up to them. There was no way out of our prison.

"Who are our attendants?" said Ari.

"Priestesses? We're meant to be in sanctuary." And I was proved right when a couple of hours later, after we'd scratched round every corner of the rooms, the door was unbarred. We quickly sat on the couches to make it look like we hadn't stirred.

A woman came in – a glint of weapons flashed on the guard behind her. I gasped. Were they to protect us? Or to stop us getting out?

Ari stood up, as haughtily as she could manage. "Leave us," she said to the guard; and the guard, apologetically, retreated.

I recognized the woman – she'd passed the barley to Myrrah before Myrrah had sacrificed the bull. She didn't smile at us or talk, but placed a tray of sweet-smelling foods and a jug of warm unmixed wine on the low table, before bowing slightly, and leaving. The bars clicked shut behind her.

"This is worse than I thought," I said to Ari. "Do you think – do you think that Timon and Myrrah are planning some kind of coup as well?"

Ari nodded. "I thought that – or began to think it – when Andro died. I felt sure Timon had instructed Aegeus to send Andro to his death. I thought he'd leave the door open for Athens to attack us. But then we went off to conquer Athens, and it didn't fit…"

"Unless," I said. "Unless that was always part of his plan."

Ari looked up, sharply. "To get rid of Andro, clamp down on Athens, give Myrrah human sacrifices for her shadow gods and leave the whole of the Middle Sea without a protector…"

"And now they're trying to get rid of us – or get us out of the way until they've succeeded in their plot – and they've held Aster over Minos and Pasiphaë all this time. They've been pretending to heal him, but really they've been preparing for his death."

After we'd eaten, and gone round the rooms once again, seeking for any sort of exit – concealed passages, chinks in the door, anything – we both sank into the couches. It was still, and we could hear nothing, only our own breathing.

Until we heard the shouting.

"What's that?" But I knew. It was like something alive, that sound, full of anguish and horror. It seemed to go on for a long time, to fill out the space of the world, pressing in on us.

"The first sacrifice," whispered Ari. She'd guessed as well. The first two Athenians, a girl and a boy, sent into the New Temple – the labyrinth – to be slaughtered. I thought of Daphne, the girl with the flaming hair. I thought of Theseus, gleaming and smiling. What plan did he have to stop all this? He couldn't have come so willingly without some kind of back-up. Could he? My thoughts were rolling around my mind, dizzying me.

The screams lasted a few more seconds. And then there was nothing.

Fear and terror coiled in me. Being trapped in that space made it worse. For some reason I could not even bring myself to embrace Ari for comfort. The fact that I was alive and imprisoned made their deaths all the more unbearable. And there were still more to go. All to feed Myrrah's plans...

With the screams haunting me, time in those rooms stretched out. I couldn't sleep that night, and the next day I avoided Ari when food came in.

All that day I was listless. I kept to my hard bed. And then, at the same time as the day before, the screaming came again. This one was high-pitched and lasted longer, so much longer than the one before. Afterwards there was sobbing, and then silence. Please don't be Daphne, I found myself thinking. Let her live. Let us find a way to save her. And the rest, said another voice in my mind. And the rest…

My dinner stuck in my throat that night. My lips were parched, even when I drank. Now I was not sure when I was asleep and when I was awake; whether it was Ari that drifted into my room and spoke to me, or some image or phantom of her. Sometimes I just rolled over and curled myself up into a ball and pulled the covers over my head and looked into the blackness, thinking that maybe destruction wasn't so bad after all.

The next time I heard the screaming, it was so bound up with the other times that I wasn't sure how many of them there had been. But something about it tugged at me so deeply that I snapped upright from where I'd been lying on my hard bed. My head felt fuzzy. I splashed some water from a bowl over my face, and rinsed it on a piece of blanket. It was difficult to stand, but I managed it, and then, as I took a few steps, my confidence grew. I came out into the main chamber. There was Ari with her hands on her hips. I looked away from her. She came up to me and hugged me, and that was all she really needed to do.

"Look," she said. "We have to get out of here. Otherwise everything we love will go."

"But how?" I said. "How can we do anything?" It was hopeless. Everything had already gone. Our parents, deceived and distant, our brother killed, another almost dead. We were all but dead too.

"We've got to get out of this!" she yelled. The next thing I knew, she'd flung the whole jug of water over me.

I coughed and spluttered.

"I've got a plan," said Ari. "But it will mean... it will mean breaking the code. We cannot let Myrrah destroy us."

"I don't think any of that matters any more," I said. Priestesses were inviolable – but we'd been imprisoned by one who was dangerous – surely we had to do all we could to stop it?

She explained her plan to me, and I started to feel crazy. It could work. It really could. "Yes!" I said. "Let's do it…" Things started to become solid in our minds.

The priestess wouldn't come back to our chambers until the next morning, so we decided to try to rest.

I found it impossible. My hard bed I didn't mind so much, but the room was airless and I kept dipping in and out of a horrible, dream-haunted sleep in which walls slid open and closed and great rivers of blood flowed. Aster, bemused and crying, was standing in the centre of a strange, giant structure, and above him was Myrrah, poised with her knife, and now Aster had a bull's head, and the knife was coming down, and now Aster would die.

Dawn couldn't come quickly enough.

And when it did, Ari and I were ready.

When the door opened, and the priestess came through, I was lying down on the couch, not moving. The priestess called to wake me. I did not stir. Behind her the guard waited, at ease. My gaze was blank. The priestess clucked her tongue and muttered something, then put the tray down and came towards me. I held my breath. She spoke gently into my ear.

I started to thrash about, moaning like Aster, and I caught the edge of her shoulder, which was enough to send her flying and the guard to come towards us.

"Hey now," said the guard, "enough of that…"

He came into the room. Ari, from behind, with a movement as quick as a swallow, hit the guard round the back of the head with a jug. He stumbled, and I took the opportunity to leap on him and disarm him, while Ari held down the priestess, her hand over her mouth.

"Don't squeal," she said.

The guard was still stunned from the blow, face down on the floor. I was sitting on his back; I'd got his sword pointed at his throat.

"You two are going to stay quietly here," said Ari.

The priestess tried to bite her, but Ari was stronger. The guard was limp beneath me. I tore off a strip of my cloak and gagged him, then bound his hands behind his back. When I was sure the knot was tight, I dragged him, still at knife point, to a pillar, and with another strip of material, tied him to it.

The priestess was floundering like a fish pulled out of water. I rushed over to help Ari, and bound up the priestess as softly as I could. Between us, we dragged her to a place in the other chamber.

Their absence would not be noticed until noon. We had until then to get into the New Temple, free Aster and confront Myrrah in front of Minos.

Ari had the priestess's veil, but I was more difficult to disguise: though not everybody in the palace would recognize my face, it was almost certain somebody would. I slid my ring off, and put it in the pouch at my belt, then put on the guard's armour and helmet. If we kept to the sides of those dark passageways, hopefully nobody would challenge us.

A fugitive in my own house, in the palace of the kingdom I was heir to – my heart raced. We cautiously opened the door. There was a passageway in front of us, quite narrow, with no sign of anybody on either side. It was, thankfully, barely lit.

We pulled the heavy door shut behind us and barred it, hoping that nobody would decide to come and see how we were doing. But Myrrah, with her connection to the darker powers – could she somehow know we had escaped? Who knew what demons she had at her command if she had the desire to call up a shadow god?

We walked briskly, Ari leading us through as many byways and back ways as possible. I kept my head down. Voices brought the first test – a group of men, lounging about. They glanced curiously at Ari, who floated past them as if they weren't there. I kept my eyes straight ahead, grateful that I was armed. One of them whistled at Ari, and I fought the urge to challenge him and carried on.

I don't know how long we were in those passageways. It felt like for ever, walking quickly, but not too quickly, so as not to attract attention. Cooks on their way to the storehouses called greetings, and chaffed me for not replying. Ari pressed on, undeterred. Each time we came across a group of people I scanned their faces, gripping my sword, my heart leaping.

At last we came to a small wooden door, somewhere on the side of the palace nearest the New Temple. Behind it was an unused chamber, said Ari; beyond that we could get out to where Aster was through a rarely used outer door. We waited for a pair of young servants to skip round the corner – I thought of Bansa, and hoped he was all right – then pushed open the door. The room beyond was empty. I shut the door, and leant against it, and took off my helmet, panting. My hair was wet with sweat. My whole body felt limp.

Not far now. All I could think of was Aster, trapped like a beast, and a sick kind of anger that filled me.

But soon he would be free, and we could stop all the slaughter.

Movement to my left. There was somebody in the shadows, a large shape.

"Show yourself," I said. The figure moved forward. And a voice, an oily, soft voice, came to my ears.

"Ah... the royal children of Minos. Out of sanctuary I see. Myrrah will not be pleased."

A plump man shuffling forward. His glistening brown face came into a patch of light, lined and worn, his eyes tired. My chest filled with rage. Timon.

16

Twists and Turns

"Traitor!" I hissed, through my teeth.

"You are only a boy yet," said Timon. "Thirteen summers."

"I am tall for my age," I said. "And stronger and quicker than you."

I put my hand to my sword. Ari, leaping forward, restrained me. I could not kill an unarmed man. But he was so vile.

"I have lived longer than you," said Timon. "And I know more than you. Who's to say I could not use my wits?"

I pulled my sword out. But Timon just stood there, a look of great sadness passing across his face.

"You have escaped, then," he said. "You found out about Myrrah's plans?"

"What do you know about them?" I said. Ari held me back.

"I know enough, Prince," said Timon, moving further forwards. I edged back, afraid of him and what he could do. Perhaps he too was in league with some dark power. The shadows around him… "I know enough," he continued, "to know … that I want nothing of it."

This was not what I expected. "You're lying," I said.

"Liar!" shouted Ari. This time I had to restrain her. "You sent Andro to his death! You…" she lunged at him, arms flailing, and I dragged her back.

Timon bowed his head. "I did not send Andro to his death. That was Myrrah's doing. But I should have realized she was up to something… At the beginning I thought Myrrah was working for the good of Crete. She was experimenting with sacrifices – at how to make the perfect sacrifice. I believed this would bring power and glory. A new age for our land."

All those carcasses by the Black Lake, I thought.

"I thought we could influence the gods, could make things better… But she had other things on her mind, things she learnt from the shadow gods… She said she needed humans to complete the sacrifice, to bring the shadow god to earth, so there would be no more need for prophecies – the gods would do her bidding, and she would control the earth. It was then I started to hate her. She went into trances, always talking to the shadow god. I think the shadow god started to take over her. How could she hope to control something that strong?"

He paused, sighing deeply. I was suspicious of him still. What were his motives? Why would he want to give up so quickly?

"There's more," he said. "She... she has power over your parents, and over Daedalus."

"I know," I said.

"What form does it take?" Ari asked. "Myrrah's power. Over our parents."

"I... I hardly wish to say."

"How do we know you're telling the truth?" I said, my hand on my sword again.

"I am loyal to the house of Minos," said Timon, and for a moment he looked like he must have looked when he was young, and my father first entrusted him with his position.

"Prove it," I said, and pulled out my ring from my pouch. "Kiss the ring, and swear on Minos and Crete, that you are loyal to our house, and that you will help save Asterius."

Timon, wobbling a little, knelt. He reached out for my hand, and kissed the ring. He said, in a clear tone,

"I, Timon the Steward, am loyal to the house of Minos and its heirs; I am loyal to Crete; and I will help save the Prince, Asterius."

When he'd finished I paused for a second, looking down at him. He seemed calm. I glanced at Ari, and in that look we both agreed that he must be telling the truth.

I grasped his hand and pulled him up, and then he clasped me. "Oh Prince," he said. "These times have been out of joint..."

"We have to act quickly," said Ari, cutting in. "We have to rescue Aster now, and stop Myrrah."

"We can't," said Timon.

"Why not?"

"Minos will not believe you. Myrrah has told Minos and Pasiphaë that she is going to cure Aster with these human sacrifices. She has been drugging them too..."

So that was it. That was why Pasiphaë would not talk to me, why Minos was behaving so erratically.

"Myrrah has something else over Pasiphaë too."

"What's that?"

"The bull story – your mother and the bull, I mean – that was all her concoction." Timon coughed delicately. "But, like most rumours, it had some basis in truth..."

"What?" Flames of rage licked through me. "How dare you!"

"Wait, Prince. I do not know how to say this. In that… in that your mother…"

"Oh…" said Ari. She put a hand to her forehead. "Daedalus."

"Your intuition is correct, Princess," said Timon.

"Explain to me!" I said, although the truth was coming into sharp focus.

"Queen Pasiphaë," said Timon, carefully, "did once have an affair with Daedalus the craftsman."

"So… Aster?"

"Asterius is your father's son – don't worry about that."

I remembered the little boy, holding a figure of a man with wings, in Daedalus's rooms. "Icarus…"

"Yes," said Timon. "Icarus is her son. Pasiphaë and Daedalus both wanted to keep him. She passed off her pregnancy as a miscarriage."

I was shocked, all through my body. But there was no time to dwell on it now.

So that was it. Myrrah knew about Daedalus and Pasiphaë – and the penalty for adultery in Knossos was severe. If my mother's adultery were exposed, she would be banned from the sacrifices, and exiled from the kingdom... We would never see her again.

"So," said Ari carefully. "If we can't do anything now, what do you suggest?"

"Myrrah has pronounced that the full cycle of sacrifices will take seven days. We have had five. She plans to send Theseus and Daphne as the final pair; then she will kill Asterius, and the shadow god will manifest fully."

"But Minos and Pasiphaë won't believe that she'll kill Aster until they..."

"Until they see it for themselves," I finished for her. They would have to witness her, in all her blackness, holding the blade above the neck of Aster. We had not stopped the slaughter. The rooms were filling with blood. "We must save him."

"Now," said Timon. "It will be hard, and it will be dangerous. Myrrah has powers beyond those we have seen." He shuddered. "But you are the heirs to Crete. And, for the safety of Crete, will you come with me?"

Ari was upright, proud, her veil torn away from her face, her eyes gleaming. I straightened up. This was our only hope. What else could we do? "We'll come with you," said Ari.

"Then follow," said Timon, and we went with him into the further bowels of the palace, ready to meet the horrors that fate had made for us. Ready to kill, ready even to die, to save our brother, our parents and our country. A monster, Myrrah had foretold, and death.

And I was ready for both.

17

Inside the Labyrinth

We were in Timon's inner chambers, He was rooting about, and found two nondescript black robes, of the sort that waiting women or minor priestesses might wear.

"I shall tell Myrrah that you tried to escape, so I decided to keep you under close observation and in confinement in my chambers," he said.

I lifted my chin, and gazed at him carefully. Crafty and subtle – perhaps he had something hidden up his sleeve.

"She will trust me to deal with you. She spends most of the day in a trance, communing with her god. Then she enters the New Temple for the sacrifice."

"What does she do?" asked Ari.

Timon looked grave. "I'll show you," he said, his voice trembling a little. "But before then... There's somebody you have to see. Come with me."

The room seemed sumptuous for somebody who was about to die. But perhaps that was the point. The prince, Theseus, was standing with his back to us, facing a tapestry of a stag at bay, and around him the dogs ready to tear him apart. The hunt goddess was at the side, looking on. The stag had been a man once, before being turned into an animal because he'd spied on her as she bathed.

Theseus turned as we entered. Timon waved away the two attendants – young men of the court. I was wearing the robes of a priestess, veiled like Ari, so they barely looked at us, smiling at the steward as they left.

"Timon," said Theseus with civility, but I could see the distaste and distance in his eyes. "Do you come to console me? Or to laugh at the captive Prince of Athens."

Timon lifted his finger, and Ari and I took off our veils.

Theseus raised his eyebrows, trying to prevent himself from showing too much surprise. He stepped towards Ari. "Such beauty," he said, "can only be found in the royal house of Minos. Princess." He kissed her hand, lingering. Ari blushed.

Again I noted how much taller he was than me, more handsome, with black hair, pale cheeks and flashing blue eyes. I wanted to hate him, but somehow

I couldn't. He let Ari's hand drop, then took mine, and bowed low.

"Your house is older and greater than mine. It is a shame that we have to meet in such circumstances. But when this is all over, we can hunt in the forests together." He gestured at the tapestry.

"What do you mean?" I said.

"I mean that I intend to slay this Minotaur of yours, and escape back to Athens. Half man, half bull, they say. Eats babies, they say. I'm not going to let an abomination like that kill me. And when I have destroyed your monster then I will return to Athens before taking my revenge on the house of Minos, ancient though you are." He looked proud and angry, and I was suddenly afraid of him.

"But why is it that the royal children of Minos come to me in disguise? I had heard that you'd been put into sanctuary whilst the sacrifices are going on…"

Timon came forwards, puffing a little. "We are here to ask your help," he said.

Theseus raised an eyebrow.

"My help? You've come to ask me to throw myself at the Minotaur's mercy? To betray my country?"

"No!" I couldn't help it. "There isn't a monster. It's all a lie, Myrrah made it up. There is no Minotaur."

"We need your help," said Ari, cutting in over me, "to stop Myrrah. She's holding my brother Asterius captive. He's a small boy but she's pretending he's a monster. But Asterius isn't dangerous – she is. She is going to call up a terrible shadow god, powered by your sacrifices and the death of Asterius, something so powerful that it could destroy Crete and Athens…"

Theseus faced us squarely. "Say I believe you. So you want me to do what?"

Timon held out a hand. "We want you to put an end to this. To… to slay the cause of the problem. To kill Myrrah."

"She is a priestess!" said Theseus. "She is inviolable!"

"She has twisted things out of all recognition. She has herself violated the precepts of her priesthood, and so deserves to die."

"But the Furies… You cannot risk unleashing them?"

"You would slay a boy, but not a woman?"

"I didn't know he was a boy."

"Come with us," Timon said, "and you will see."

Three cloaked and veiled priestesses followed Timon a little later, just as it was beginning to get dark, in the direction of the New Temple. The two armed soldiers at the entrance sprang apart when Timon arrived, standing to attention.

Inside the palace we could hear the sounds of shouting from the feasting. By now I knew that sound. They were ready for sacrifice. I hoped that Minos and Pasiphaë were not joining in.

Entering the New Temple was to enter a darker world. There was a long corridor ahead of us. To our right was a door, which Timon opened. "We can watch from here." He looked at me and Ari. "What you're going to see won't be very... pleasant. But you must see it, you must know what she is like."

"I can see it," said Ari. "If my brother has to endure this, then I can endure it too."

I nodded my agreement, feeling sick inside. Aster was only little, and ill. He didn't know what was happening to him. He should be playing with his wooden toys, not being used as an instrument in someone else's plans.

We set off. Turns left and right, corridors everywhere, never knowing what direction I was going in, then up a flight of steps until at last we were in a smallish room, looking out over a much larger one. The sight was something so extraordinary I took a moment to understand it. A series of passages, all interconnected, but leading apparently nowhere. The lines. I understood now. The labyrinth.

Above us was the temple roof. Torches shone at intervals along the passageways, so the whole was lit with strange shadows. There were many dead ends. Looking down on the labyrinth from above was like looking at a complicated pattern in an embroidery. I felt lost and confused even just staring at it. In the centre was a raised platform, surrounded by sputtering flames.

Tonight was the sixth night of the sacrifices. I felt something like I'd felt when I'd seen all those dead animals by the Black Lake, as if a dark power was scratching away somewhere. "The Athenians will come in after the feast," whispered Timon.

Theseus remained calm, silent; Ari too. They were standing close together, Theseus's hand making its way to Ari's shoulder. She let it stay there.

Not long passed before the temple doors were flung open. Outside it was dark, but the outlines of the doors were visible in the torchlight. Two Athenians were framed in its space: one girl, one boy. Theseus stiffened.

The boy and the girl walked calmly forward. They disappeared for a moment from our view, then came back into it, looking so small and vulnerable.

"Pallas," said Theseus. "He is a good friend. The girl is the daughter of my father's best general – Philoclea. She has the sweetest voice in all Athens, and is a better shot than me."

I liked him a little better for that. But nothing could stop the tension building in my guts.

When Pallas and Philoclea reached the end of the passageway that led into the labyrinth, they stopped, looked at each other and clasped hands. Then they separated, Pallas going to his left and Philoclea to her right. I wondered what they'd been told – that they were about to meet the Minotaur, the half-man half-bull that had already become a legend, the monster that ate human flesh?

As if reading my mind, Timon said, "They know that their companions haven't returned. But they think that if they make it through to the other side of the labyrinth, and the exit, they can live. At least, that is what they have been told."

"We can't just watch them die!" I said.

Pallas was walking steadily down a passageway, in and out of the light from the torches. He did not seem to falter, but strode on, choosing his turns without thinking. Philoclea was standing at a crossroads, deciding which way she should go. Then she turned one way with resolve. But something rumbled, and a wall slid backwards, barring her way. She backed away in the direction she was forced to go.

Myrrah, I thought. There was some kind of system to shift the walls of the labyrinth, making it ever more confusing, moving Philoclea and Pallas always closer to the centre. "Pulleys," Daedalus had said, "the walls will slide…" It's not fair, I thought. They're not even being given a chance.

Full of rage, I turned to Timon, thinking blindly that I could run out, warn them, end it all.

Timon held me back. "What can you do?" he whispered. "You must see it happen. Then we can see her weaknesses, and plan how to show Minos and Pasiphaë and rescue your brother. You need to see how it works, to be prepared." In the flickering light I could see his fleshy lips; spittle hung from them, and he wiped it away. Was this all a trap? Had he lured us here only to kill us?

Down below us Pallas and Philoclea were struggling in the lines. Whatever they'd been expecting, I imagined, it hadn't been this.

More or less at the same time, they reached the passageways adjoining the centre. A hatch in the dais opened, and a platform rose up out of it. I'd heard of such things in the east: Daedalus must have learnt about them from the travellers who sometimes came to court. They said their king would sit on a throne that rose into the air to intimidate petitioners.

A strange shape rose up on the dais. Small in the body it was, horned, and when it came fully into the bright torchlight, I saw, shifting in and out of the shadows, the sight of a bull's head, bristling and huge.

So there is a Minotaur after all – the stories were true. A sick feeling spread upwards from my stomach.

No... it was Aster, Aster in a bull's-head mask. His arms were held down on either side of him, his head slightly bowed. What on earth had Myrrah done to him?

Pallas and Philoclea came to either side of the dais. When they saw Aster they both paused. I knew what they were thinking. Was this the monster they were so frightened of?

"It's just a boy with a mask on!" Pallas called.

Aster didn't move.

"Be careful, it might be a trap!" Philoclea said, as Pallas started to climb up the dais.

"That's no monster," said Pallas, scoffing. "I could take him down with my little finger!"

Don't hurt him, I thought. Please don't.

Pallas bent down to look at Aster. "He's only a little one! I can see him through the mask!" He put his hand out. "I won't hurt you," he said. "Show us the way out!"

Philoclea clambered up to stand beside Pallas. "He's frightened of you," she said. "Let me try!"

As she moved forward, a scratching sound heralded the opening of concealed door in the wall behind Aster.

Myrrah was there, tall and robed, holding a long spear, and on either side of her two priests with swords leapt forward, and though Philoclea managed to dash out of the way, Pallas was caught by the edge of a blade and stumbled; Myrrah hurled her spear at Philoclea, and it caught in her flank as she was turning to run.

The scratching sensation grew stronger in my mind, something like a rat scrabbling at a wall. Something wanted to get in – or out.

I didn't cover my eyes. I had to see. Pallas and Philoclea were being tied up, screaming the screams of those about to die, those who have nothing left for them, like we'd heard for five nights in a row from our prison. Myrrah sprinkled them with wine and barley, then stood above them with her knife. And I saw her blade plunge into them, one after the other, again and again.

Their blood poured into the passageways beneath, pooling into a small puddle. Something clicked, and I shivered. It's a machine, I thought. What Daedalus said. The labyrinth is a machine, powered by sacrificial blood.

"Aster!" I whispered. He stayed calm – maybe, like my parents, he'd been drugged. I hoped so, for his own sake.

When Myrrah finished, the bodies were left where they lay. Myrrah and the guards departed, taking Aster with them.

Theseus was standing rigid; fury was blazing in Ari's eyes. I felt sick.

"No," said Timon. "We must stay a little longer."

The scratching sound was surrounding me, now coming from inside and outside of me at the same time. I wanted to wash it away, but I knew that I couldn't. It was like a swarm of bees had collected in my skull. I clutched my head.

"You have to watch," said Timon. "It is not finished."

A darkness encroached around the edges of the dais, making the stage smaller and smaller. It formed itself into something like the shape of a man, but far, far bigger, towering above the dais, seeming to suck in everything around it.

It leant forward to where the bodies were. How lifeless and still they looked now, Philoclea's blond hair spreading out behind her, Pallas like a wooden doll.

The shadow reached out a limb, sniffing over the bodies, creeping, stretching. I blinked, the sickness in my stomach. It looked like the shadow was feeding on the corpses.

Within moments the bodies were gone. And so was the terrible form, leaving behind it the empty dais.

I ran to Ari. She held me, as if I were little again, as if I wasn't Prince Deucalion Stephanos, heir to Crete, the boy on whose shoulders the fate of his country rested, but just little Stephan who'd grazed his knee. I put my head in the crook of her shoulder.

Timon muttered something, but I didn't hear it. I didn't care any more. Nothing seemed to matter. That blackness destroyed everything it touched.

But as Ari held me, things shaped themselves in my mind, out of the darkness, into real, living images. I saw all of Crete in ruins. I saw that shadow, enveloping, destroying. Who knew when it would stop? Who knew what it could do to make its power stronger?

I couldn't allow this. I was going to stop Myrrah, bring her to justice. I am Prince Deucalion Stephanos, I thought.

And I will save Crete. I am going to stop the shadow god, return the land to safety, even if I have to die doing it. And I felt the shape of my future forming into a double-headed axe.

18

The Perfect Sacrifice

Tonight was the night of the final sacrifice, when Theseus would die. The tapestries on the walls of Timon's room hemmed me in. I couldn't taste the wine that Timon gave me, couldn't eat the herby bread, the olives or the roasted meats. Ari was pacing up and down the room, her hands behind her back, her chin jutting out, her eyes flashing. Timon was sitting down, his hands folded in his lap. I was sitting down too, my legs crossed, my hands held tight together, feeling the shape of things in my mind. We were all trying to work out how to thwart the evil that was to come.

Theseus had gone to his room – his prison. He would tell Daphne what he knew, and then they would be as ready as they could be. It meant she could survive. If *we* survived...

We had to save them. If Theseus and Daphne died, then next Myrrah would kill Aster and bring the shadow god into our world.

"Yarn," said Ari.

"What?"

"Yarn. When we get in there…"

"First of all," I said, "what do you mean 'we'? I'm going in on my own."

"We're all going in. Theseus will be in there with Daphne, as sacrifices. They'll be going in through the front passage. You and I will go round the back. There must be a way in for Myrrah – we saw her leave the dais, remember? We'll find a way to come up behind her – then, as she's about to strike, we'll leap in and tie her up."

"What about the guards?"

"Theseus and Daphne will deal with them."

"What about the shadow god?"

"That…" said Ari. "We will have to deal with that when it happens … and just hope."

"Hope?" I said, glancing at Timon.

"That's all we have," said Ari. "Look." She walked over from where she'd been standing by a table, picking at some newly picked grapes. "You're my brother, more than anything else in the world. Aster is my brother too. There is no Andro now. These people have reached into our hearts and torn something out. They're trying to break everything. We have to put ourselves through this. We have to. Otherwise we don't deserve to call ourselves children of Minos."

"I know," I said. I was feeling it too.

Timon coughed. "I have to go and prepare your parents," he said. "You know what to do? I will take the King and Queen to the New Temple when the feast is over and the moon is a fourth part of the way up the sky."

Ari nodded. "We'll be fine."

"Good." He looked at us, held our gazes. "My children," he said. "May the Mother Goddess watch over you and help you." He bent to kiss our foreheads, then waddled off, an odd hero.

It was time to get ready. Theseus would enter the New Temple in an hour. We had to be prepared for anything. And I knew now why I needed the Double Axe. I knew, too, that it was my gift – but I'd had to find it myself. I knew why Ari needed her blade and Aster his gift.

"Where's your gift from the People of the Mountains?" I asked Ari.

She lifted up her tunic, and there, girded around her waist, was a purple sheath gilded with strange figures.

She pulled out the short sword, the knife gleaming with light that seemed to come from elsewhere.

"I feel the mountain people in it," she said.

"I need to fetch the other gift from my chambers," I said. "Come with me." Disguised and veiled, we slipped out into the passageways. Outside Timon's room were groups of people – serving men, clerks, standing around waiting for the final feast. But there was no sense of celebration.

"Unnatural…" one of them was muttering, a thin man. "Unnatural…"

We moved through them like shadows ourselves. Nobody gave us a second glance.

My chambers were unlocked, and empty. I went straight to the chest and opened the lid. There was Aster's package, as I remembered it.

And there, gleaming and strange, was the Double Axe.

I hurriedly picked them both up, and we set out again.

Ari hid Aster's package under the folds of her robe. The axe was harder to conceal. I held it to my side, which meant that I had to walk a little stiffly. Outside it was cool. The stars looked down upon us and I remembered Theo telling me about them. Were they really people, turned into flaming lights? I sent up a prayer to them. If there's anybody up there, I said, please help us.

Most of the people in the palace were at the feast. They would not be allowed in to the New Temple to watch the offerings take place. I could hear their noise in the distance.

Ari was trembling. I think she knew, or guessed at, what would have to happen. When we came round the corner of the compound and saw the New Temple rising in front of us, white and cold in the early moonlight, she stumbled, and I held her. She shook me off, and carried on without saying a word. The hoot of an owl rang out, while above the bats swooped low, darting here and there.

It was difficult to walk with the axe, and I could barely keep up with Ari. When we reached the back of the New Temple we paused behind a screen of low bushy shrubs. Four heavily armed guards stood in front of the door. And behind that, who knew how many more?

The moon was rising higher. Timon would now be leading my parents from their chambers to the New

Temple – drugged and stumbling, probably, their eyes blank and their minds fogged.

"We need to think fast," said Ari. She tapped her finger against her teeth, a habit I'd never liked. I shifted the Double Axe, feeling the power in it, the coolness and the strangeness of the People of the Mountains.

"We can't run straight at them – we'll be hacked down before we even get to the door," I whispered. The guards were thickset men, holding spears, with swords at their waists and probably a knife or two about them as well. They looked like they had been ordered to kill. And more.

They shifted and stamped their feet. The moon was now breasting the top of the highest point of the compound, gleaming on their weapons. Timon would be leading Pashiphae and Minos through the main entrance now, with a guard of honour, seating them at the feast as if they were complicit in all this. But I knew they weren't – they couldn't be. Those drugs had addled their minds.

We had to act – and I just ran out. I didn't really know what I was doing.

"Stephan!" Ari hissed.

But I was acting on instinct. I came into a patch of moonlight in front of the guards. They raised their weapons.

"It's a priestess," said one of the guards.

"What's she doing out here?" said another. "Myrrah said nobody to come in!"

"What's wrong with her?" said the first.

I stayed very still, and hoped that Ari would realize what I was doing. She must have done – her footsteps sounded behind me. The guards approached. "Here's another one. Lonely, are you?"

Ari inclined her head, and I did the same.

"Hey boys!" said the first guard. "Looks like we've struck lucky here…"

There were three in front of us, and only one remaining at the door. If my plan didn't work, we'd be dead on the ground in a second. I was breathing so tightly I was almost dizzy.

The first guard ran his finger under my chin and grinned. Through the gauze of my veil he looked monstrous, his breath, hot and unpleasant.

Another touched Ari's shoulder. And then – maybe it was the power inherent in the weapons, or maybe it was some deeper connection between us – we both withdrew our weapons and struck at the same time.

Ari stabbed one in the side of his chest, and spun round to get the other unawares in the back. Meanwhile I had hefted the axe. At the last minute I faltered, and instead of cutting at the guard, I struck him on the head. He fell. The other guard was running towards us. We went at him and circled him. He seemed frightened, and young.

He made a lunge for Ari, who sliced at the backs of his legs with her dagger. He dropped to the ground, blood oozing from the wounds, crawled a couple of inches towards his brother soldiers, then lay still. We ran into the back of the New Temple. We had to evade detection, find Myrrah and follow her until she got to the dais. Then we would reveal what she really was.

There seemed to be no more guards in the passageway. No rooms led off it. It went straight into the centre, towards the labyrinth, the lines.

My mother and father would be approaching the New Temple doors now. Theseus and Daphne would be ready: Theseus, maybe stamping his feet, slapping his hands together, and the beautiful flame-haired girl, Daphne, who I might never see alive again.

A change in the air temperature announced that we must be nearing a larger room, cooler and darker. There were no torches, and my eyes hadn't yet become accustomed to the darkness.

Ari put out a hand to stop me. I crashed into her and listened: Myrrah's voice, chanting. My eyes began to peer through the darkness. There was a ring of torches up ahead, where Myrrah was kneeling down. Around her were a group of people – priests or guards or both, it was hard to tell.

From Ari came a sharp intake of breath. I followed her gaze and saw Aster sitting on the floor, slightly apart. He was playing with something – with a horrible tug at my heart, I realized it was the wooden toys I'd given him.

In the dimness Myrrah was kneeling in front of an opening. It must face onto the labyrinth. My heart missed a beat – Daedalus was at her side. So he was in on this too. But then, next to him, his son Icarus, and just behind Icarus's neck, was the point of a spear.

Myrrah stopped chanting. By now I could see her quite clearly. She made a signal to Daedalus, who nodded. He patted his son on the head, as though to say, don't worry, I'll be back. Icarus, frightened, held on to his father's hand; the guard pulled him back.

Daedalus moved to a position by Myrrah where there was a system of levers and pulleys. This must be what controlled the walls in the labyrinth, I thought. As a priestess brought in the bull's head, Myrrah beckoned to Aster, who came quite meekly. He gurgled, and Myrrah laughed. That made me feel sicker than anything. She gently took the wooden toy from his grasp, and placed the mask on him. She's making him feel important, I thought. It's not fair.

She pushed Aster out through the opening, and he went to take his place. We could see him from the back, lit by a circle of torches, and the way the shadows fell on him looked monstrous.

Theseus and Daphne must now be in the labyrinth. Daedalus, peering into the darkness, was almost certainly watching them carefully. That's why the passageways were so well lit. Every now and then he pulled a lever, with remarkable ease, no doubt manipulating his precious pulley system that he was so proud of. Inside the labyrinth, the lines, the walls would be moving, pushing Theseus and Daphne ever closer to the centre.

Then suddenly Myrrah stiffened. Ari and I shrank back against the wall as she raised herself up. I'd forgotten how tall she was. She stepped forward.

"She's going out to meet them!" Ari whispered in my ear. "We have to move now!"

She was right. I held the Double Axe tightly in my hand. There was nothing else for it.

"If we edge round the room we can try to sneak in without the guards seeing us," she whispered.

We set off as fast as we could, our left hands touching the smooth stone of the walls. The guards, clustered around Daedalus, didn't seem to want to watch what was going to happen. Three priests – all of them armed – were gazing out at Aster.

Myrrah stepped onto the dais. For a moment her shadow blotted out everything. I could not see what she did. A girl screamed – Daphne! – and my heart sank. Then Theseus – a shriek of pain.

Myrrah moved in towards Aster, her sword uplifted. She was two paces from him; then one. Bending down she whispered something into his ear, and he knelt down. She faced away from us, holding out the sword above her like some avenging goddess.

"Minos!" she shouted. "Pasiphaë! The sacrifices have been made…"

So she had killed Theseus. Things began to fall away in my mind.

"It is time to purify your son! It is time to purify the world! I will call the shadow god… I will control the world!"

Myrrah held the sword above Aster's head. And suddenly I heard shouts – from Minos, from Pasiphaë and Timon.

"Now," said Ari.

And we ran, as fast as I've ever run before, faster than Swift, faster than the wind. The guards didn't notice us until we'd reached the opening. Without stopping, we jumped across and into the centre of the dais.

It took a moment to adjust. Everything was shadow. There was Theseus, on his back. Daphne lay on the floor, her flaming hair spread behind her head. There was Aster, kneeling, shaking, as Timon and my parents, horrified on the balcony, reached out.

"Father!"

Myrrah turned round and shrieked.

"You will not stop me!" she cried. "The shadow god is almost here…" She lunged towards Aster.

Ari rushed in front of her and held her blade at her.

"You think that's enough?" said Myrrah.

Pasiphaë and Minos were standing up now, Pasiphaë clinging to the edge of the balcony. "My child! My children!"

Aster, at his mother's voice, took off the mask.

"Asterius!"

He stood up and started his low moaning, urgent and unmistakeable.

"Myrrah!" Minos roared. "Priestess or no priestess, I command you, in the name of my kingship, stop! Guards! Seize her!" But the guards, terrified, shrank back. Where was Daedalus? Nowhere to be seen. He'd probably hustled Icarus away the moment he could.

Myrrah laughed, while at her feet Theseus and Daphne groaned, struggling to get up. Snatching a sword from a guard, she took Aster by the arm, and, still laughing, leapt over the edge of the dais with him into the lines of the labyrinth.

I could feel the blackness, feel that terrible shadow welling up just outside the world, strengthening itself, ready for the blood of a prince of Crete, ready for the blood of Minos, the blood of the House of the Double Axe.

This was it, then. I bit my lip, and tried to stop the tears as the walls went sliding once more. And I prepared to meet the end of everything.

19

FIRE AND FLIGHT

"Stephan! Stephanos!" The voice came as if from far away. Ari was holding something out to me. "Brother! We have to follow her. Come on!"

It was a ball of yarn. She tied one end around a post. "Tie the other end to your waist!" she said. "Then we can always follow it back to the beginning."

I knotted it round me as tightly as I could.

"I'm coming too," said Daphne, her side bleeding heavily. She pressed Ari's fabric to the wound. With her other arm she was holding up Theseus.

"And me," said Theseus. "We must rescue your brother."

"You're too hurt," said Ari.

"If you think," said Daphne, "that a little scratch like this can put me off, then you've got to think again."

Theseus came towards Ari and embraced her tightly. He didn't seem to mind, and nor did she, that he was bleeding on her. "We will get out of this," he said.

"And I will take you back to Athens with me, and you will be my queen."

Ari looked at him levelly. And then she kissed him, and laughed and turned away.

"Come on, Stephan!"

From above came shouts. "She's going to the northeast!" shouted Minos.

"This way," Ari said grimly, vaulting over the edge of the dais. She turned to look back at me, strong and brave and true. Theseus and Daphne followed.

I gritted my teeth, and ran to the edge, and jumped down to join them, the yarn spooling out behind me. The way ahead was dark, and the way behind was bloody. We were in the lines that push and shape our lives. We grasped hands, and gripped our weapons, and strode forward as Pasiphaë screamed above us. The walls shook; the torches flickered. And so we entered the labyrinth.

As soon as we got into the first passageway, everything else fell away and the darkness was intensifying. Ari grabbed a torch off the wall, but its flame seemed almost without illumination.

"Wait!" I said. "Where are Theseus and Daphne?"

She shone the torch round – nobody there. We couldn't hear Minos or Pasiphaë any more. I shouted, at the top of my voice, "Daphne!"

A faint echo, coming back to me, was swallowed up in the thickness of the silence.

"They've gone…" said Ari, and for the first time she sounded frightened.

"Or maybe we've gone…" I said.

Laughter, the laughter of Myrrah. We froze.

"Come on," said Ari.

"But how will we find Myrrah?" I said. "Or the way out?"

"The yarn," said Ari. "Just make sure it doesn't break."

The walls towering above us seemed so huge and forbidding, as though they'd always been there. It was hot. I could feel my skin prickling with sweat.

"Sshhh…" I said. Footsteps – it sounded like two people – echoing in the darkness. And Aster, moaning.

"This way," said Ari. I kept as close to her as I could, the Double Axe heavy in my hands.

We turned a corner and came into a small enclosure, and Ari halted. I almost ran into her.

"Back," she hissed. There was a bright, shimmering light ahead of us.

"What is it?"

There, standing in the centre of the enclosure, was something I never thought could exist. A being made out of flame – shaped like a person, but spitting and hissing like a bonfire, and moving like liquid.

It saw us. I could feel the heat coming off it. I started to sweat. Ari stood as if she'd been turned into stone.

"Ari!" I shouted. "Ari! Run!"

We were too late. The fire creature was on us. It roared, and I felt my hairs singe and my face scorched by the flames.

"Ari!"

She put up her arm instinctively and I ducked, trying to evade the overwhelming heat. But then I looked up. Ari was holding up a shield – black and unembellished. Aster's present. Its wrapping of leaves and bark burnt away.

The shield made an invisible barrier that seemed to encase us in a bubble. Flames licked around the edge of it but couldn't reach inside. The creature wailed in frustration. A demon, I thought, a demon of flame. It crackled and lashed at us, the force of the blows striking the barrier, smoke and vapours coming off it.

"Move slowly now," whispered Ari. "Keep behind me." We edged around the fire demon. It hissed at us, reaching out tongues of fire. I slashed at it with the Double Axe, coming out from behind the barrier, and felt the searing heat of the axe connecting with something solid. Something real and alive was moving underneath all the heat and flame.

Bolder, we stepped further forward. I swung back the Double Axe, feeling my skin blister, and struck the flame demon with all the power I could summon. My blade lodged so hard in its flank that I struggled to get it out. It clawed at the Double Axe, but I retreated back behind the shield's barrier.

The demon flared again, making itself larger and more hideous. The power of the shield seemed to be weakening, and my hands shook with pain from the heat.

"Move on!" shouted Ari. We pushed forwards.

The being gave a roar. Then, like a candle guttering in a draft, it billowed out sideways and slowly shuddered, in and out of existence – there was nothing left but a charred husk, looking horribly like a human body.

"Keep going," said Ari. "I heard Myrrah's laughter ahead."

We ran on, smouldering yarn being drawn out behind me.

The blackness thickened. We could barely see ahead of us now, and I didn't dare to look behind. Footsteps seemed to be coming from more than one direction.

"Which way?" said Ari. We stood at a crossroads.

"This way," I said, and we ran onwards, straight into a dead end. "Keep the wall on your right and we'll try again," I said, and we set off, running as fast as we could, the yarn spooling out behind us all the way, until we stumbled over the charred body of the flame demon lying on the ground.

"We've gone backwards…" said Ari.

"How?" I said. "We haven't doubled back on the yarn!"

"Then something else is going on…"

"Away!" I shouted, and we turned and ran again.

Ari's sense of direction was failing her and the yarn didn't seem to be working. All we had was the echoing sound of footsteps and Myrrah's shrieking laughter. Maybe she'd already reached the centre of the labyrinth, and maybe she'd already killed Aster.

Maybe the shadow god was already in this world…

"Over there!" As we passed an entrance to a passage on our right, I caught sight of shifting figures passing not far ahead of us. "They've gone that way!"

We turned and entered the passageway. Myrrah's laughter sounded nearer, and I swore I could hear Aster's groaning as well. Was he trying to help us? My heart quickened. Maybe we could find him. He groaned again, louder this time. "This way!" I shouted, and ran on, Ari following.

Then I heard something strange for the inside of a building: wings, beating the air. A disturbance, like the faintest of breezes.

Something swooped down at us, skimming over our heads. I looked up. There was nothing there.

Wings flapping, and again something came towards us in the darkness. Ari's torch lit up for a second a ghastly figure – a huge freakish bird – but it was a man's face, staring and white, now making those horrible squawking calls. My whole body shuddered. Ari and I went back to back, her shield above her head. But the beast cawed loudly as it swooped on us, and lifted the shield with its claws with such force that Ari had to let go, and it flew off, dropping it a few feet away from us.

It laughed, a horrible, cackling noise that reminded me of Myrrah. In the gloom I could see its white feathers as it landed on a wall above us. It was mocking us. But we had our weapons. My axe gleamed, and Ari drew her sword.

It launched itself up into the air again, and circled around us. Then it dived towards us. We were ready.

The first time we both missed it, and a sudden hot pain gripped my shoulder. Its claws had got me. Blood was streaming down my arm.

I steeled myself. Once more the creature settled on a wall, gazing down at us and making that awful raucous sound. It flapped its immense wings. I shivered, nursing my shoulder.

The creature readied itself to swoop once more. I whispered to Ari. "Wait till it's almost on us. Then step apart and…" I left the sentence unfinished. She'd know what to do.

It shifted from claw to claw, and turned its head on one side, then another. What did we look like to it? Where did it come from?

The weight of the Double Axe was making my shoulder hurt even more. Sweat made my grip slippery. I begged the Mother Goddess not to let the weapon drop out of my hands as I hefted it. And I prayed to the People of the Mountains to help us.

The beast spread its wings, and cawed. In a moment it was in the air, coming towards us, and its wings were the world, and I waited, standing my ground, till I could see into its eyes, eyes that showed nothing but ancient coldness and cruelty. I stepped forward, so slowly, and Ari stepped away, and it flew between us. We spun on our heels and as it came to the lowest point of its dive we smashed our weapons down onto its back, deep into its foul body.

It let out a shriek, so human it reminded me of the cries of the dying Athenians, and fell, in an ungainly mass, bleeding, to the ground. It cawed, pitifully. Ari grabbed me.

"We have no time to waste."

We moved on, deeper into the lines.

"This way," Ari said, her face pale in the shifting torchlight. By now I didn't know how long we'd been in the lines. Hours? Sometimes it felt like we'd only been in there for a brief moment. Time itself was changing.

Strange sounds came from the passages around us. Singing, chanting, other sounds deep and old. Surely we were moving towards the centre of the labyrinth, while who knew what was happening in the world above. Somehow we'd slipped into another layer, behind the surfaces we could normally see. A place where the shadows were stronger, where fire demons and harpies could thrive. Theseus and Daphne were nowhere to be seen, and the cries of Minos and Pasiphaë had long since faded away.

Round and round we went, the darkness encroaching and vast. Sometimes it felt like we were battling against a huge headwind. Other times we sped along as if we were at the races. Always it was the darkness, a thing in itself, making us go on and on as though it would never end. I saw myself and Ari, stumbling on for ever, never reaching any light, never finding Aster.

Hope was ebbing away, little by little. Darkness without end. We would be food for the shadow god soon enough.

At last we turned a corner and came into a larger space where the walls, black and smooth, seemed higher. And here in the middle...

"Aster!"

Standing alone and vulnerable with that abomination of a bull's mask on his head, there was nothing around him, nobody, no sign of Myrrah, no guards, no beings. Aster!

I ran towards him, blindly, hope rekindled in my heart. I called his name, enveloped him, and felt him limp in my arms. Ari came behind me. We put our weapons down.

"Aster!" I shouted again. "Asterius?" Releasing him, panic once more knocking at my mind, I grabbed hold of the bull mask and pulled it off.

20

The Shadow God

"Steph!" Ari sounded terrified.

Lights flamed and the space was lit up. Underneath the mask a blank, wooden face stared up at me. I flung the crude doll away from me in horror. It landed with a thud – and there, several paces behind it, tied to an altar, was Aster, moaning and shaking. Above him, holding two swords, was Myrrah.

Before we could even scream, the blade was falling, cutting into Aster. This was the darkness at the edge of the world, and I felt its hunger and its need.

I ran towards that altar and I launched myself at Myrrah, knocking her clean over. She screeched. The darkness was stronger than ever, wild and angry.

I held Myrrah down as she thrashed underneath me. Ari was untying Aster. He was alive, but bleeding. She grabbed him and dragged him with her to a corner. She thrust the shield at him – what was she doing? – and he held it uncertainly.

Myrrah was kicking. I could hardly hold her. She was powered by a strength that seemed to come from somewhere else. The shadows were shifting and changing. She lunged and bit my wrist, and I yelped and let go of her left hand. She raked her nails across my face and reached for the sword she'd dropped. Within a brief instant, she was on her feet, wielding the sword.

Where was the Double Axe? I glanced round and saw it lying a few feet away. Ari was behind me, crouching, as if to jump.

"Move and I'll kill him," shouted Myrrah. "One Cretan prince is as good as another. The blood of Minos is what we need, the old royal line, the true blood of Crete, the blood that comes from the god of the sky!"

The edges of the space were blurring.

"He is coming," whispered Myrrah, her eyes glinting with fanatical fire. "The shadow god. The king of the shadows! He is coming to give his power to the world… We will not need augury any longer. There will be an end to the future! We will know all things!"

A shape was beginning to form. That horrible thing I'd seen before, that had taken the bodies of the Athenians.

The shadow god was manifesting, folding itself into a shape like a man, but huge and terrible, with a face carved out of rock, and eyes that were lit by crimson fire. There was something on the god's head, like a crown, made of blackness, and his robes fell around him like thunderclouds as his body rippled with lightning. A tang, a sharpness was in the air, like just before a storm.

Myrrah grabbed me, dragged me round to face the shadow god. I could feel her trembling with joy as the point of her sword pricked my neck, and blood welled out.

The shadow god gazed at us with a blank, terrible stare. What had those eyes seen? The souls of the dead passing before them, in all their numbers... The sword went in again, deeper this time. With her other hand Myrrah was clutching my wrists together.

She yelled exultantly. "Oh Prince of Darkness! You have come to us!" She bowed, and pushed me down before her.

The god made a rustling noise, like a thousand birds leaving their roosts. I could feel its hunger.

"I bring you the final sacrifice. A royal prince! The heir to Crete, of the line of Minos, and a descendant of the sky god himself! The eldest! Is it not even better than the other?"

The god's hands were almost on me. He was going to envelop me, consume me, destroy me as my spirit ebbed away.

Then a low, soft moaning sound – a sound I didn't think I'd hear again. And it was coming nearer.

Something small and frail butted its way past Myrrah and in front of me. Something – or someone – holding a shield. As I blinked and struggled, the shield began to glow, and some kind of light and power came from it.

The god stopped.

Aster's face behind the shield was grim and fixed. He was moaning as loudly as I'd ever heard him moan. And the shield was not just a shield. It was a weapon, too, projecting a force that was protecting him and me.

Slowly we edged backwards. The sound of the god rang in our ears like waves thundering through a cave. Myrrah was screaming.

Somebody took my hand. It was Ariadne. She held her sword, and gave me the Double Axe.

And the three of us came together.

The god roared, but a power came from us, made of light and strength and beauty. Something whole. I remembered the three mountain people dancing round the pyre: the trees, the stones, the water.

The power from us grew. It pushed against the shadow god. His eyes flamed red, his nostrils flared. But I no longer felt afraid. This was my family, these were my siblings.

"Go back," I shouted. "Go back to the world below!"

"Go back!" Ari joined in, and Aster yelled, his face and body straining.

The shadow god rumbled like a mountain on fire. It tried to reach around us, to slip its fingers under the shining carapace that we made. But it couldn't.

The shadow god was shrinking. I swung the Double Axe and felt it strike something. There was something there that could be hurt, and destroyed, like the flame demon, like the harpy.

It began to pull itself into its blackness.

I was beginning to feel weak. Aster too was faltering. Even Ari beside me was moving more feebly now. I still had the yarn, tied to my belt.

"We have to keep going," I said.

The god was lapping at us. Its freezing power was getting to me and its shadows were growing stronger again. My eyes started to close. The world seemed to go sideways. Everything started slipping away.

And I saw. I saw the world where the shadow god came from, a howling emptiness. I saw the hungry spirits prowling the vast spaces below. Nothing grew, there was no light. I saw why it needed us, why it needed our blood. I saw dark mountains and deep pools and huge, eternal loneliness.

But we could not give in. I opened my eyes again. How could I give in? Not now. I looked at Ari, fighting with her last breath. Aster, pressing forwards, ready to die himself. And I gathered my strength. I lifted up the Double Axe, the symbol of my family, of my country.

And I sliced at the shadow god's head.

With a sound like an avalanche, the thing groaned and scrabbled at its neck. The light from our weapons grew brighter.

It started once more to shrink.

But as it shrank, it cast wildly around, sending out shoots of darkness, like an octopus lashing out with its tentacles. And it found something – Myrrah, standing, undefended, by herself, screaming and railing. It grabbed her with a tendril of its fading body, and rumbled in something like triumph as Myrrah's screams filled the air and everything shivered and shook.

"The prophecy..." she said. "My prophecy..."

"It was no true prophecy," I shouted. "You lied to us. In you the darkness lies. That's what the woodman said. But the prophecy came right in one way. The monster is here. And the death you saw in me is yours."

And then the walls of the labyrinth started to shake once more. "The thread!" shouted Ariadne. "Follow the thread!" I pulled Aster in front of me. We went as quickly as we could, along those falling passageways. We were going back to the light, out of the darkness, out of those twisted lines. Just follow the yarn.

That was the last thing I remember thinking.

Just follow the yarn.

And then a wave of darkness washed over me.

21

The Children of Minos

I opened my eyes, seeing smoke and light, and my mother's face looking down at me. She was smiling. I stretched my hand out to her and she held it. She smoothed down my cheek, and handed me a goblet, which had some rich, strong drink in it that smelt of spices. I gulped it down, and coughed. It burned my throat, but in a good way.

I was in my own bed. I sat up, gently. "Careful, Stephan," said my mother. "Don't tire yourself…"

"Aster!" I said. "And Ari!"

"They're fine," she said. "You must rest. You'll see them soon enough."

"Aster." I said. "He saved us."

"I know he did, my darling," said my mother. "I know he did."

And then I slept once more. In my sleep I saw things I didn't understand: a boy with a jewelled necklace and a dark man in metal armour; a blond man in red and a snake; I saw women with golden faces; I saw beasts with horns and staring eyes.

And I saw the face of the shadow god, which looked like my face, and then like Myrrah's, and then like the faces of people in dreams.

When I woke again, Aster was sitting on my bed. He was playing with his wooden toys: the bull, the man and the horse. He was making the horse gallop across the bed, and the man was chasing after it. When I sat up he laughed, and rocked backwards and forwards, and patted me awkwardly on the head. I hugged him.

"Asterius," I said. "You are the true prince. You saved me, and Ariadne, and all of Crete."

He laughed again. I don't know if he understood me, but he looked at me with eyes that flashed for a second with something. And then he went back to his toys.

"You look awful," came a voice. In the doorway Ari was dressed in a long blue gown edged with gold, and around her head was a garland of white flowers. "You've been ill for a week."

A week of troubled dreams, of not knowing, of strange images in the darkness.

Theseus came into the room with her, limping slightly. He rested his hand casually on Ariadne's arm, and she lifted her own to squeeze his hand, and there was no mistaking the smile that she gave him.

"You were very brave," he said. "All of you." He smiled and came towards my bed, clasping my hand as he knelt by my side.

"What happened?"

"It was as though the labyrinth started to collapse," said Theseus. "We couldn't see you any more. We were in there with you, or so we thought, but there was no sign of you. It was like you'd disappeared from this world."

"I think we did," I said.

"Daphne and I couldn't find you anywhere. I couldn't see anything. And then everything started shaking. We ran, back to the dais. At last I saw you all – the three of you, exhausted, stumbling along, and you came out onto the dais and collapsed. And then the walls crumbled and we carried you out."

"The whole temple fell in?" I said. Daphne, I thought. He'd said Daphne.

"No, just the labyrinth walls."

"And… was anyone hurt?"

"Daphne wasn't with me when I came out," he said. "But there are still people looking…"

I looked away from Theseus, focusing my attention on a small patch of light on the wall. "And Minos?"

"He wants to see you. Both of you," said Ariadne. "Can you walk?"

I nodded. Light was streaming through my window, and outside the birds were singing. I could taste peace.

"Back to work again," came another voice. "No rest for me then…" Bansa's familiar laugh. "Suppose I'd better help you get ready then, hadn't I?"

For the first time in a long while, I laughed, the joy coming up from my stomach and filling my whole body.

When I'd got changed, I found myself in the Great Hall, standing before my father and mother, who sat on their thrones, splendid in white and gold and purple. Timon was sitting on the second step. He smiled and nodded at me, and I nodded back. He lifted his hand and made a little bow. Daedalus stood by the side, his hand resting on the head of his little son. My half-brother, I thought. There were guards on either side of Daedalus, and as he caught my eye I knew he was sorry for his part in the labyrinth.

And there was Theo, wobbling on his stick, muttering under his breath to his friends. The Great Hall thronged with people.

Minos called for silence. "My sons," he said. "My daughter. Come forward!"

Aster came with his nurse, a little bit confused, so I smiled at him, and touched his shoulder. He was holding the figure of the bull. Ari came towards us, tall, her blue gown shimmering.

My father and mother stood up. They came to the front of the dais, holding hands.

"People of Crete," said Minos. "We have been under a curse. The false priestess Myrrah confounded us with poisons and lies. She wanted power. But that power would destroy us all. My princes – my three princes – were brave, and saw the truth of things. Before all Crete, I give thanks. I give thanks to my bold son, the Prince Asterius, who from henceforth will be known as the Shield-sword!"

I nudged Aster forward gently, and he went up to the dais, a little dazed, a little sideways. My parents placed their hands on his head, and then set a golden circlet on him. He touched the strange thing and gurgled, then sat down happily on the step.

"I give thanks to my daughter, valiant and strong, the Princess Ariadne, who from now will have the title Sword of Crete!"

Ari, blushing, went straight up the steps, bowed and took off the garland she was wearing. Pasiphaë replaced it with a golden crown, which gleamed and shone in the light.

"We shall be happy, too, to have the Prince Theseus as our son as he joins the Sword of Crete in marriage. There will be an end to war with Athens, and peace in the Middle Sea!" He gestured towards Theseus, who stood, alone and proud, tall and handsome. He bowed his head, and smiled at me.

"And my eldest son, the heir to Crete. Worthy of that name is he. I give thanks to the Prince Deucalion Stephanos, the garlanded one, who will be known as the Double Axe."

Cheers rang through the hall. Somewhere trumpets blared. My shoulder still ached, but I didn't care. The crowd took up the cry. "The Double Axe! The Double

Axe!" And I walked up towards my parents, who looked down on me with love in their eyes, and I bowed before them, feeling the weight of a golden crown descending on my head. I held their hands, and faced the mass of people, my people, thinking, I am the Double Axe, and I will fight for you always, whatever comes our way, and I will keep you from all dangers, and help you live and prosper for as long as I am alive.

We feasted for three days. And on the third day we married Theseus and Ariadne. Bansa was an attendant, and he scattered flowers and nuts in their way, and I joined in, and Aster came after, grinning widely. My mother and father walked sedately behind, arm in arm.

And behind them, walking with the help of a stick, was the flame-haired girl, Daphne. She'd been found, bruised but alive, in the rubble of the labyrinth. She flashed me a smile, and I nodded back at her, and caught the nut she cheekily threw at me.

Things were normal again. At least, I hoped they were. I said as much to Bansa as, on the fourth day, we slipped away from the wedding celebrations to go and walk in the woods. It was beginning to get cold, and I was wearing a thick fur tunic. Bansa had come out without warm clothes, and was pretending not to mind.

We passed into the forest. The trees shivered, as though the presence of the People of the Mountains, just briefly, touched me in my heart; and then it was gone. Thank you, they seemed to be saying. Thank you.

"If you *think* you're hot," said Bansa, trembling, "then you *are* hot." He rubbed his hands together and blew on them.

A group of young courtiers walking nearby were talking excitedly. "You know," exclaimed a tall, dark-haired boy I knew from the hunt – "Theseus slew the Minotaur with one stroke! But not before the monster ate all those Athenians... There were skulls and bones everywhere when he went in!"

"How do you know?" said one of the girls, laughing and shaking her head.

"I saw it! I went past the temple and I saw the shadow of the Minotaur! I saw his horns and I went in afterwards and I slipped in the blood of the sacrificial victims!" said the boy, sounding so convincing I almost believed him myself. "I saw the bones on the floor! I saw the Minotaur's body!"

"But I thought it was the Prince Asterius…"

"No no," said the boy. "He was being held captive, by Myrrah. Myrrah was going to feed him to the Minotaur. But Theseus saved the day!"

I smiled to myself and wondered if Theseus had something to do with this story. The boy pulled out a ball of yarn. "I found this in the ruins! Ariadne gave it to Theseus so he could find his way back."

The girls clustered round him, ooh-ing and aah-ing.

How could I change what was already taking on a life of its own? Or was it better for people to think that some imaginary monster had been killed? It would make them believe that things were safe.

It would mean that nobody would hear about how near we'd come to total destruction.

Bansa made a face and pulled me away, and together we climbed up the hill above the palace, looking down at the lights as the evening crept along. The sun was slowly setting, sending out a last scarlet blush to the darkening sky. In the near distance by the shore was Theseus's ship with its black sails, in mourning for those who would be killed. Soon Ari was going with him, to Athens, away from our lives, to another court, to another self. Perhaps I would never see her again.

"You will," said Bansa.

"Will what?"

"See your sister again."

"How do you know?" I looked at the stars above us, so distant. The constellations Theo had taught me about had all fled my memory.

"You'll see her again now," came another voice.

"Ari!"

"Your nurse told me you were up here." By her side Aster lunged up like a puppy, before settling himself at our feet, playing unconcernedly with a toy, the winged man that Icarus had when I'd met him. He must have given it to Aster.

I smiled at Ari. "We're looking at the stars," I said.

"There's the snake," she said, pointing at the constellation. "And that one... I don't know."

"It looks like somebody kneeling down," said Bansa.

"So it does," said Ari.

So we knelt down, and prayed to the Mother Goddess to thank her, and to the People of the Mountains, and then we sat watching the sun sink down into the night, as a procession of people went bearing things to Theseus's ship – cups, plates, all sorts of royal gifts.

Then Ari said, "I have to go now. We are sailing with the tide, early in the morning."

Aster made a sound – that familiar low noise. I stroked his head as the ship's sails billowed in the breeze and the moon's silver light skimmed the sea.

One by one, the torches by the ship flickered and went out. Ariadne smoothed down her long, blue silk dress. She kissed me, lightly, on the head, and stroked my cheek, then pressed her hand against Aster's back.

And we walked down the hill into the night.

THE END

ACKNOWLEDGEMENTS

To my agent, Philippa Milne-Smith, and her assistant Elizabeth Briggs; Elisabetta Minervini, Mike Stocks, Christian Müller, William Dady, Clémentine Koenig, Thomas Storey, Alessandro Gallenzi and all at Alma; and to all who kindly read and commented upon various drafts of *The Double Axe*, including William Bingley, Robert Christie, Magnus McCullough, Tatiana von Preussen and Tom Williams.

Photo: Tatiana von Preussen

Philip Womack is the author of *The Other Book*, *The Liberators* and the *Darkening Path* trilogy. He has loved Greek myth all his life. He lives in London with his wife, son, lurcher and pet minotaur. (The latter may not be true.)